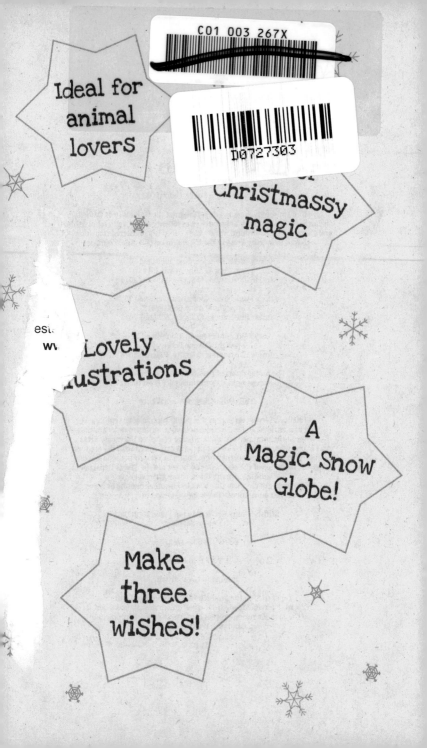

Ideal for animal lovers

Christmassy magic

Lovely illustrations

A Magic Snow Globe!

Make three wishes!

OXFORD

UNIVERSITY PRESS

Great Clarendon Street, Oxford OX2 6DP

Oxford University Press is a department of the University of Oxford.
It furthers the University's objective of excellence in research, scholarship,
and education by publishing worldwide. Oxford is a registered trade mark of
Oxford University Press in the UK and in certain other countries

British Library Cataloguing in Publication Data
Data available

ISBN: 978-0-19-276877-3

1 3 5 7 9 10 8 6 4 2

Printed in Great Britain

Paper used in the production of this book is a natural,
recyclable product made from wood grown in sustainable forests.
The manufacturing process conforms to the environmental
regulations of the country of origin.

LUCY'S MAGICAL WINTER STORIES

Written by
Anne Booth

Illustrated by
Sophy Williams

OXFORD
UNIVERSITY PRESS

Contents

LUCY'S SECRET

REINDEER

Written by
Anne Booth

Illustrated by
Sophy Williams

OXFORD
UNIVERSITY PRESS

To Mum and Dad
-Patrick and Anne Simms-
who always made Christmas so special

Chapter One

School had finished, the Christmas tree was up, and the fairy lights were twinkling. Dad was busy hanging tinsel, paper chains, and Christmas cards in crisscrossing cheerful lines across the room. He had the radio on loudly and was singing along to the Christmas songs. Dad loved the Christmas holidays.

Mum was in the kitchen, making Sunday lunch. Lucy's big brother Oscar was lying on the sofa, playing video games, and Lucy was sitting at the table, writing her letter to Santa.

'There isn't any point in writing to Santa,' said eleven-year-old Oscar, who had got bored with his game and was looking over her shoulder. 'You're eight, not a baby.'

Lucy was just about to get very cross and do something very unChristmassy to her brother when, luckily, Mum stuck her head around the door.

'Oscar, can you help me set the table?' she asked. 'And Lucy, can you go and tell Gran that lunch is ready?'

Lucy was glad to go and get Gran, and quickly put on her wellies and coat. As she closed the door behind her she could hear Oscar complaining loudly about being made to do all the work while Lucy wrote stupid letters.

Lucy crossed the lane and went down the little garden path to Gran's side door.

'Hello, Gran!' Lucy called, as she pushed the door open and stepped into the kitchen.

At one end of the large room was a big kitchen range and a dresser with

pretty patterned plates and cups on. There was also a sink and a cosy armchair with patchwork cushions. But the other end of the room was like a little animal hospital. There was a row of cages for injured or sick animals, and there were shelves stacked high with all sorts of animal food, biscuits, and mealworms. Lucy knew the cat food was for the little hedgehogs Gran found in the winter which were too small to survive the cold and hibernation. On the big wooden kitchen table in the middle of the room was a set of weighing scales, but instead of weighing flour or sugar Gran was weighing a hedgehog.

'Hello, Lucy, darling,' Gran said. 'Is lunch ready? Just let me write down Brian's weight. I think he's heavy enough to be put out to hibernate soon. He's over 600 grams—isn't that great?'

As Gran popped Brian back in with the other little hedgehogs she was feeding up, Lucy checked on the rest of the animals. A little red-breasted robin with an injured wing was hopping around a big cage, and a rabbit with a bandaged paw was asleep in another. As soon as the wild birds and animals got better Gran would set them free, although the very little hedgehogs would stay in the warm with her until spring.

Gran washed her hands and put on her coat to walk over to Lucy's house. They closed the door and left the birds and animals sleeping safe and sound.

Lucy could hear the sound of plates and cutlery being laid out on the dining table when she and Gran arrived. Dad took Gran's coat while she admired the decorations, and then they all went through to the dining room and sat down. Mum had lit some candles and it felt as if Christmas was getting very near. Oscar stopped being grumpy and told Gran all about the football team he wanted to get into and the karate classes he had started. Now that he was in Year Six, it seemed to Lucy as if he didn't want to come after school and help with Gran's animals any more.

'Mum, please can I have a stamp for my letter to Santa?' Lucy asked, after they'd finished their pudding. 'I need to post it today so it gets there in time.'

'Only losers write to Santa,' muttered Oscar.

'Oscar!' exclaimed Mum, shocked.

'Don't be mean, Oscar,' Dad said, looking very hard at him.

'What a strange word to use,' Gran said, thoughtfully. 'Why do you think Lucy is a loser, Oscar?'

'Writing to Santa's a babyish thing to do,' Oscar said, sulkily. 'And anyway, it doesn't work. Lucy asked for a horse and she got a rocking horse. Even last year, she didn't get the puppy she asked for.'

'Maybe Santa didn't think Lucy was old enough for a puppy last year,' Dad said.

'I'm sure he did his best with the presents,' Mum said. 'Lucy got a very nice pyjama-case dog. You love Scruffy, don't you, Lucy?'

'I do love Scruffy, and I'll write to Santa and tell him,' Lucy said. 'I'll ask him if he needs any help with anything, too.'

'What a lovely idea, Lucy,' Mum said.

'I'll do the washing up, Emma,' Dad said. 'And I'll cook the rest of the meals this week—and help with Christmas dinner! It's nice to be home from work and able to help out for a change,' he added, getting up from the table.

'That would be the best Christmas present of all,' Mum said, and Dad made her smile by holding some mistletoe over her head to get a kiss from her.

'Yuk!' said Oscar and Lucy at the same time, and everyone laughed.

'There's a stamp in the drawer, Lucy,' Dad said. 'Maybe Gran can go out with you to post your letter to Santa. Oscar, you can bring the dirty dishes into the kitchen with me.' Oscar opened his mouth to argue . . .

'I mean it,' Dad said, firmly, and Oscar started collecting the plates.

Chapter Two

Lucy drew a picture of a reindeer on her letter to give it a proper Christmassy look. She gave it to Gran to read before she put it in the envelope.

Dear Santa

I would like a kitten for Christmas.
I don't want a horse or a dog in case it
hurts Scruffy or Rocky's feelings. They
think they are real. But please can the
kitten be really real this time? Gran says
to tell you that I have been helping her
all year, and she thinks I am ready for a
pet. This year I have fed the hens, and

the rescue guinea pigs, and the rescue
rabbits. I have helped with the baby
hedgehogs and a fox Gran looked after.

　　　Lots of love from
　　　Lucy

P.S. I know you must be very busy at this
time of year, but I'm on holiday now
and can help you if you need me. Here
are some pictures of the animals I have
looked after this year:

'Lovely!' Gran said, and gave her a hug.

Lucy put the stamp on the envelope and addressed it.

'It isn't only losers who write to Santa,' she said to herself. She hoped Santa hadn't heard Oscar. He could be so rude.

Gran took her hand as they walked to the post box, and it made her feel safe and Christmassy again. She closed her eyes and wished very hard as she posted her letter, and she thought she heard the sound of sleigh bells chiming. It made her feel tingly inside. When she opened her eyes something wonderful had happened— snowflakes were falling all around!

Somehow she knew deep down that Santa would get her letter and read it.

'Do you think Santa will ask for my help, Gran?'

'I don't know, Lucy, but I'm sure he appreciates your kind thought. And if he doesn't need you, I certainly do! There are lots of animals who need help at Christmas.'

'Gran, do you think Oscar will be all right?' Lucy asked, as they walked back home in a world that was getting whiter and whiter. 'He hasn't written a letter at all. What if he doesn't get anything from Santa because he has been so rude?'

'Don't worry, Lucy. I'm sure Santa understands. He knows Oscar has a kind heart really.'

Lucy wasn't sure about that. It seemed like a long time since Oscar had done anything kind for her.

Oscar was in a much better mood when they got back, and Gran stayed and they all played Monopoly together. Snow kept falling steadily all afternoon, covering ordinary hedges and walls with white magic. Lucy looked over at Mum and Dad laughing together.

'Dad, can we go sledging this Christmas?' she asked.

'Yes! I've got a whole week at home

with you—so let's do lots of fun things!'
Dad said.

Gran set off home just as it was
getting dark. She put so many layers on
Dad teased her that she was as plump as
Father Christmas.

'Grandma Christmas,' Oscar said,
and Gran laughed and ruffled his hair.
She was the only one who was allowed
to do that.

'I want a drum kit for Christmas,' Oscar said later that night, when he and Lucy were in the bathroom brushing their teeth.

'Have you written a letter to Santa?' Lucy asked.

'Not exactly . . . ' Oscar replied. Suddenly he flicked the water from his toothbrush at her and ran off to bed before she could get him back.

When Lucy had finished, she went into her bedroom. 'You're going to meet a new friend soon,' she told Rocky. 'I've asked Santa for a kitten, and I think this year he might think it's the right time.' Her rocking horse

rocked back and forth thoughtfully, his eyes kind and brown, his fur gleaming in the moonlight. She could almost hear his soft whinny. He really was a beautiful horse. Scruffy looked up at her from her bed, and she knew that if he could, he would wag his tail. She did love them.

'Sweet dreams, you two,' Lucy said as she got into bed and lay down, cuddling Scruffy.

'Sweet dreams, Mum,' she said as her mum came in to close her curtains and kiss her goodnight. 'I'm going to dream of kittens.'

'Why do you say that?' Mum asked. 'Have you been talking to Gran again?'

'I've been writing to Santa. I've asked for a kitten and told him how I've helped look after all Gran's animals this year.'

'Lucy, love, don't get your hopes up too much, will you?' Mum said, as she

kissed her cheek. 'We don't always get what we want but I'm sure Santa will do his best.'

Dad came in then and sat down on her bed.

'Sweet dreams, Dad. Hope you dream of kittens,' Lucy said. 'Then you'll know what Santa is bringing me.'

'What colour kitten do you want me to dream about?' Dad asked, very seriously.

'I don't mind, as long as it loves me,' Lucy said.

'How could any kitten not love you?' Dad chuckled, and ruffled her hair the way Gran did.

'Goodnight, Lucy!'

'Goodnight, Dad!' Lucy replied.

Chapter Three

Lucy woke to the sound of sleigh bells, which faded away as she sat up. She rubbed her eyes. It was still night-time, and everything was quiet. 'I must have been dreaming,' she said to herself, but she felt awake and excited and she didn't know why. She got out of bed and opened the curtains. Outside the window, the snow was falling in white swirls. Inside the room suddenly felt magical, with tiny stars sparkling in the air. As Lucy watched them, the stars formed into letters.

'Look under your pillow, Lucy!' the stars spelled out in front of her.

She turned and saw something white sticking out from under her pillow. She drew it out. It was an envelope addressed to her, and the stamp had a picture of Santa on it. As she looked at it, Santa seemed to wink at her! Lucy blinked, shook her head, and looked again. Santa on the stamp smiled and nodded at her, and then the stamp stayed still again. Dazed, she opened the envelope. The white paper she took out shimmered as she read the big, black, curling handwriting on it:

Dear Lucy

Thank you so much for asking me if I needed help. Nobody does that. What a kind girl you are! As a matter of fact I do need help. My smallest reindeer is not very well and needs someone to nurse him back to health before

Christmas Eve. I know you have helped look after your gran's rescue animals, so I am asking you to do this very important job. Go down to the garden shed and you will find him.

Thank you, Lucy. I am relying on you to help me. I have to have all the reindeer well or I won't be able to deliver the presents. Starlight may be small, but he is a very important part of the Christmas team. He shows us where to go, and without him we'll never find all the children's homes in time.

But, Lucy, this is TOP SECRET!
That's why this letter will
disappear as soon as you finish
reading it.

Lots of love from

Santa

Lucy rubbed her eyes to check it wasn't all just a dream, but there they were—the envelope and the letter on her bed, twinkling and glowing.

'Look, Scruffy! Look, Rocky! A real letter from Santa! I have to look after one of his reindeer!' She picked up Scruffy. She could almost feel him wriggling with excitement in her arms. Then there was the sound of sleigh bells again, and the letter, the envelope, and the smiling Santa stamp disappeared, leaving just a cloud of stars that glittered and faded.

'I wish I could have shown that letter to Oscar,' Lucy said to Scruffy and Rocky, as she rushed to put on her cosy red slippers and dressing gown. She tiptoed downstairs, her heart thumping, and put on her red duffle coat over her dressing gown. She turned the key in the back door and went out into the garden.

It was beautiful. There was snow on the garden path, and her slippers got a little wet as she crunched along. In the moonlight the snow looked as if it had lots of little diamonds in it, and the sparkling seemed to get brighter the nearer she got to the shed. She pushed the door open . . . But it was just a garden shed, full of boxes, watering cans, and garden tools.

I must have just dreamed it all, Lucy thought, feeling very disappointed. Of course Santa wouldn't write to me. She was just about to pull the door closed again and rush back into the house to get warm when she saw something move. Could it be . . . ? Her heart started beating faster, and she walked right into the shed up to a pile of old flowerpots and peeked over.

What Santa had told her was true! There, in the corner, was a very small reindeer. A beam of moonlight came through the shed window and fell on his soft white fur. Lucy could see him breathing as he looked up at her. This was better than anything she had ever asked for. Ever.

'Hello, Starlight,' she whispered. 'Don't be frightened. It's Lucy.' She tiptoed carefully forward, moving a bucket to the side as she went. The reindeer was only about the size of Rocky—not much bigger than a small dog. He was so little he didn't even have big antlers like the pictures on Christmas cards; just baby ones, peeping through his fluffy coat.

How could you ever help to pull a sleigh? Lucy wondered. She had never been this close to a reindeer. She'd never even seen one in real life before. This was a real, live animal, not a picture or a toy. She put her hand out slowly and felt him reach out his soft muzzle to nudge it. Gran always told her never to rush an animal when you meet it. Starlight's breath was warm but his nose was cold.

He was lying down on his side, his long legs splayed out. His big brown eyes had long eyelashes and he looked bewildered. He shivered a little.

'You're cold,' Lucy said anxiously, and edged herself forward so that she could sit cross-legged on some sacking next to him. When she felt ill the first thing her mum did was put her in bed and wrap her up so that she was cosy and warm. She looked around for something to wrap him up in. There was an old picnic rug they hadn't used since the summer, an old gardening jacket Dad used sometimes, and more sacking.

Starlight's tail wagged a little. It reminded Lucy of the lambs in the fields at springtime. She opened her coat and carefully pulled him up on to her knee, then she tried to snuggle them both under some sacking, Dad's jacket, and the rug. At first he was all long legs and baby antlers, and it was a bit tricky sorting out all the layers, but she knew she had to warm him up by cuddling him. Eventually he settled down on her lap. He was surprisingly light and furry, and just holding him in her arms made her think of stars and snowflakes and Christmas bells and the feeling you get when school finishes for the holidays.

'I wish I could take you into school to show everyone,' she said, stroking his soft fur. He sniffed and snuffled and gently nuzzled her face and looked deep into her eyes. Then he sighed, tucked his long legs up, and snuggled into her, his hard baby antler buds resting against her chest. It was a bit uncomfortable, but finally she managed to shuffle into a position against the wall. Soon the shed was full of the sound of a baby reindeer snoring.

'I can't believe you're here, Starlight,' she said, looking down at the sweetest little reindeer she could ever have imagined. 'But what should

I do now?' Starlight just wriggled in his sleep, his ears twitching. He shivered again and Lucy held him tighter to keep him warm. She knew it was up to her to get him well for Christmas.

Chapter Four

Lucy must have fallen asleep, because the next thing she knew, a small wet nose was nudging her cold face. As she opened her eyes, she saw two big brown eyes staring back at her. She was sitting on the floor in the garden shed.

The snow-bright daylight was streaming through the window and she had a real-life little Christmas reindeer in her arms. It was all true!

'Hello, Starlight!' she laughed. 'You're looking much better!' His little tail was wagging as he climbed off her lap and shook himself. He looked so sweet and small. He even tried to give a little jump! He still wasn't strong enough though, and his legs wobbled and crumpled underneath him. He shivered. Lucy took off her coat and wrapped him up in it to make a sweet little bundle. He didn't wriggle or try to get out of it, but let himself be tucked up snugly again. Lucy put him down carefully on a little nest of sacks, covered him with the rug and Dad's jacket again, and lined up flowerpots around him, partly to hide him and partly to protect him from the draught. He watched her solemnly with his big brown eyes but didn't move.

'I should put up a curtain so nobody can see you through the window,' Lucy said. 'I promised Santa I'd keep you a secret.'

Starlight closed his eyes peacefully.

'Don't you worry about anything, Starlight,' Lucy said, beaming at him. 'I'm going to get you strong for Christmas. Wait here. I'll be back.'

It was cold outside in the snowy garden just wearing her dressing gown, and Lucy was glad to find the kitchen door was still unlocked. The good news was that she could get indoors. The bad news was that she met Mum coming down the stairs.

'Hello, Lucy, love,' Mum said, surprised. 'What are you doing up so early?'

'I . . . I was a bit hungry. Um . . . do you have a carrot, Mum?'

'A carrot?' Mum laughed. 'That's an unusual breakfast!'

'I just really feel like one,' Lucy replied.

'There are some in the vegetable rack. Make sure you wash it first. In fact, you may need to peel it,' Mum said. 'I'll show you how.'

This wasn't what Lucy wanted. Starlight was in the shed alone, and here she was, washing and learning to peel a carrot she didn't even want to eat!

'You'll never guess what Lucy is having for breakfast!' Mum said, as Dad and Oscar came downstairs. 'A carrot!'

'Rather her than me,' Dad said, filling his and Oscar's bowls with cereal. Lucy reluctantly munched her carrot and tried to look like she was enjoying it. While Mum was pouring the tea and Oscar and Dad were laughing over a joke on the back of the cereal packet, Lucy edged her way over to the cupboard and sneaked another carrot out. She thought for a moment that Oscar had seen her, but he just looked away and carried on being silly with Dad. So Starlight's breakfast was sorted. Now to keep him hidden.

'Mum, do we have any spare curtains?' Lucy asked. 'I thought . . . I thought I might do a puppet show for Christmas.'

'Do you want to make a theatre?' Dad said, looking interested. 'I'll help! I love a good puppet show.'

Oh no, thought Lucy.

'That's not fair!' Oscar said. 'I thought you were going to come to the music shop with me and look at drum kits.'

'The ones with headphones,' Mum said quickly to Dad.

'Oh yes,' Dad said. 'Sorry, Lucy. Can you wait until we come back? Oscar's seen a drum kit in the music shop and we're going to try to be there when the shop opens.'

'Yes, that's fine,' Lucy said, relieved, edging her way to the door, a carrot behind her back.

'I think there's an old red velvet curtain folded up at the bottom of my wardrobe,' Mum said. 'I was planning to make something nice with it but I wasn't sure what, and I've just been too busy to get around to it. You can have it.'

Lucy went upstairs, got dressed, and found the curtain. It was perfect. The velvet was a little worn, but it was thick and heavy and nobody would be able to look through the window and see Starlight.

'I'm doing my best, Santa,' Lucy said under her breath. 'I'll keep the secret and Starlight will be well for Christmas.'

She waited until she heard Dad and Oscar go out and then tiptoed down the stairs, the curtain in her arms with the carrot hidden under it.

Mum was in the kitchen. She had her special Christmas apron on and she was making cakes.

'Lucy—here—you can lick the spoon,' Mum said. 'And once the cakes are cooked we'll decorate them for Christmas. You can make the icing and then we'll put sprinkles on them. It'll be fun!'

'Um . . . I have to make my puppet show,' Lucy said.

'There's time for both,' Mum said. 'It wouldn't be Christmas without us making our cakes together. We have to get a special one ready to leave for Santa tomorrow, like we always do. It's one of my favourite bits of Christmas!'

It was one of Lucy's favourite jobs too. She and Mum always put lots of decorations on the cakes, and leaving out the biggest one for Santa, and carrots for his reindeer, was something they always did every Christmas Eve. But today she really wished she didn't have to do it. She just didn't have time.

'Can I just put the curtain away?' Lucy said. 'I want to put it in the shed.'

'The shed? You don't have to make your puppet theatre in the shed,' Mum said, surprised. 'It's too cramped and cold and dusty in there.'

'I've . . . I've just got some surprises in the shed. For Christmas . . . ' Lucy said. 'Please don't look.'

Mum laughed. 'OK, Lucy, I'll stay away from the shed. But if any of those surprises are chocolate, don't keep them out there. I'm pretty certain there are mice. It really would be better to keep your presents in the bottom of your wardrobe. No one would look, I promise.'

But Lucy was out of the back door before her mum could stop her. 'I'll be back in a few minutes,' she called.

Lucy rushed down the path and opened the shed door. For a moment she worried it had all been a dream, but then two white furry ears moved above the flowerpots and Starlight lifted his head to look at her. He was so beautiful.

Lucy could hardly believe that she was looking after a Christmas reindeer. This was the most important job she had ever had. She wouldn't let Santa down. He was relying on her.

'I can't stop, Starlight, but here's a carrot.' Lucy put it down beside him. He stuck his little muzzle out to touch it, but didn't try to eat it.

'You must eat to get strong,' Lucy said, and stroked his soft fur. His little tail started wagging, and he nudged her hand with his head, but he didn't try to get up. He was still very weak.

'Lucy!' Mum called from the kitchen. 'Come and wash your hands and help me choose the cake decorations.'

'I'm sorry, Starlight. I'll be back soon,' Lucy said, tucking her dressing gown around him. 'Please eat your carrot. I've got to get you better for Santa.'

She put the velvet curtain down on top of a wheelbarrow. She hated leaving Starlight alone in the shed. What if someone looked through the window and saw him?

Starlight gave a little bleat.

'Ssh,' Lucy said. 'Mum's calling me so I've got to go. I'll put up that curtain later. Settle down and go to sleep. I'll be back as soon as I can.'

Chapter Five

As soon as Mum and Lucy had finished decorating the cakes Lucy ran back to the shed. Oscar and Dad would be back soon and she didn't want either of them to find Starlight.

He greeted her with a sweet little bleat and tried to get up, but he got tangled in her dressing gown and had to lie down again.

'No, Starlight,' Lucy said firmly. 'Stay there. I can't stop to stroke you. I've got to put this curtain up so nobody sees you. Mum says she won't come to the shed, but I don't want anyone looking through the window. I promised Santa I'd keep you secret.'

Luckily, there must have been curtains in the shed before, because there was still an old curtain wire, so all Lucy had to do was hook the velvet curtain over it. The curtain was heavy and Lucy struggled to get it up, but she finally managed it. Now nobody could look in and see Starlight. It made the shed very dark, though.

'I'll be back in a minute,' Lucy said. She could barely see Starlight in the dark, but he gave another little bleat. Lucy made her way to the chink of daylight showing at the side of the shed door and came out into the winter sunshine. She ran back to the house and up to her room.

Lucy found what she was looking for. It was her night light. She didn't really need it any more, but it was so pretty that sometimes she liked to keep it on at night and watch the snowflakes fall gently on the little house in the blue globe. She rushed back out to the shed with it.

'Look, Starlight. This will keep you company in the dark.' She put it next to him and the gentle light lit up his fur and made his big eyes shine. He made a soft snickering sound and she really didn't want to leave him. Mum was right, the shed was very cold. That wouldn't help him get better.

Lucy tucked the dressing gown closer around him. He sniffed her hands gently, his ears twitching. He settled down and closed his eyes as the snowflakes in the glowing globe swirled around beside him. He looked

thinner and weaker than he had been
when they had woken up.

'I think Gran might have some
little coats for the animals she rescues,'
Lucy said. 'I'll go and see if she's in. I'll
be back soon.'

Lucy ran as fast as she could down
the road and found Gran cleaning out
the cages.

'A coat?' Gran said. 'How big?' Lucy stretched out her arms.

'That's big for a toy, Lucy.'

'It's for Rocky,' she stammered.

'Well, that one was for Monty, the little Shetland pony foal I had—why don't you try it?' Gran said, pointing to a bundle on the shelf.

'That's perfect!' Lucy said, relieved. It was soft and cosy. Starlight would love it.

'Lucy, is everything all right? You looked very worried for someone just playing a game,' Gran said.

For a moment Lucy longed to tell Gran. 'No. Everything is fine.'

'Well, I'm here if you need me,' Gran said, filling up the rabbit's water bowl.

'Water!' Lucy exclaimed. 'I haven't given him water! I mean, I haven't pretended to give Rocky water!' And she rushed off back home.

Little Starlight was delighted to see her. She carefully put the soft coat on him, then the dressing gown back on top. He looked so sweet. He snuffled her face and tried to climb on to her lap.

'I've got to get you something to drink,' Lucy said, gently pushing him off. She really wanted just to give him lots of hugs, but she had so much to do to get him well.

'What are you up to?' Oscar said from behind her as she filled a bowl with water from the kitchen sink.

'Nothing,' Lucy said, and quickly tipped it out again.

'Time for lunch, Lucy,' Mum said, coming into the kitchen.

'Can I just—' began Lucy.

'No,' said Mum. 'I want us to have some nice family time and eat our lunch together. Come and sit down. Whatever you're doing can wait.'

Lucy thought of little Starlight alone in the shed and hoped Mum was right. She tried to eat her baked potato and butter as quickly as possible. Luckily, Oscar and Dad were so busy telling Mum about the drum kit that nobody noticed that she had left a bit of baked potato in the bowl. She thought maybe Starlight might prefer it to the carrot.

When Mum and Dad and Oscar left the kitchen to go into the sitting room Lucy quickly got another bowl and filled it with water from the sink, and put both bowls on a tray to take down to the shed. Then she put on her wellies, quietly opened the kitchen door, and crept out into the garden.

Poor Starlight didn't look at all well. He was lying flat on the sacks, completely exhausted. His white fur wasn't shining any more, and he looked thinner and his fur seemed paler than when she had left him. The night light was still glowing, the snow still falling in the little globe.

'Starlight,' Lucy said, kneeling down beside him. 'Starlight, please get well. Please. Look, I've brought you some of my lunch, and some water.' He raised his head to look at her, and his little tail gave a wag, but then he put his head down as if he was too tired.

'Caught you!' came a voice from behind her as a blast of cold air filled the shed. Lucy jumped and turned quickly to see Oscar standing in the doorway. 'I knew you had an animal in the shed. I saw you take the carrot this morning, and then I saw you with the water bowl. I knew you were up to something!'

Oh no. Why did it have to be Oscar? 'You mustn't tell anyone!' Lucy whispered urgently. 'It's a reindeer. It's one of Santa's reindeer and Santa asked me to look after him and get him well for Christmas, but he's just getting worse,' Lucy said.

Oscar walked in and looked past the line of flowerpots. When he saw what was in the shadows his mouth opened in surprise.

'Hey! Lucy! That's a deer. Where did you get him? You can't keep him in here.'

'I know. I told you. It's one of Santa's reindeer,' Lucy insisted.

'But Lucy, Santa—' Oscar started, but then stopped as Starlight lifted his head and looked straight into Oscar's astonished face. For a moment, the reindeer seemed to shimmer.

'What can we do?' Oscar said. He wasn't scornful anymore. He was kneeling down beside Starlight, stroking him gently, just as he used to do when he and Lucy both helped Gran with her animals.

'I don't know. I've given him food and water and a warm coat, but nothing has worked. But we have to do something, Oscar. It's Christmas Eve tomorrow!'

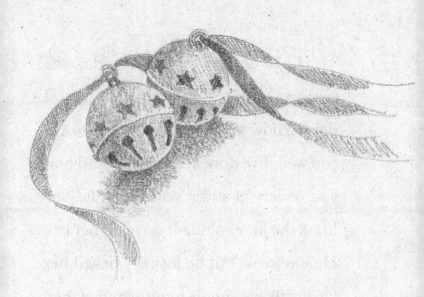

Chapter Six

Starlight looked unwell, lying on the sacks in the back of the shed. His eyes were closed and he was panting. A tear ran down Lucy's cheek but she rubbed it angrily away.

'I just don't know what to do,' she said to Oscar. 'I'm so sorry, Starlight. I don't know why Santa chose me to get you well. I've done it all wrong, and now you're very ill and it's all my fault.' She lifted the little reindeer up on to her lap. He was weak, but he lovingly licked her face with his rough tongue and sighed as he nestled down in her arms.

'Look, Lucy!' Oscar said suddenly.

There, in Lucy's arms, as she hugged him, the little reindeer stopped panting and sighed happily. His fur was getting whiter and brighter in front of their eyes and there was a soft light glowing all around him.

'Cuddling him is making him better!' Oscar said. 'That's why Santa asked you, Lucy. He knows how good you are at hugs. Maybe Starlight just wasn't getting enough love and attention. You've kept him warm and given him food and water, but maybe on top of all those things, Christmas reindeer need love, and that's what's going to get him well.'

It was true. Starlight's nose was getting blacker and shinier, and his tail was wagging more even as Lucy cuddled him. Maybe she could get him better after all. But there was still a problem.

'I can't stay here in the shed all day though,' Lucy said.

'Why don't we smuggle him up to your bedroom?' Oscar suggested. 'I'll go and tell Mum and Dad to stay out of the way. I'll tell them that I need to help you carry a special Christmas package up to your room.'

Lucy and Oscar smuggled Starlight up to Lucy's room. Though he was small, he weighed too much for Lucy to carry him on her own, so together they carried him down the path wrapped up in a big soft bundle of rug and coats. His little nose stuck out and they were glad Mum and Dad had agreed to stay in the sitting room.

'Don't look, Mum and Dad!' Oscar called, as they came into the kitchen. Luckily, Starlight kept very calm as they struggled up the stairs, Oscar going up backwards and Lucy following. Starlight's big eyes blinked but he didn't make a sound, even when Lucy stumbled.

'Slow down!' Lucy said. 'I nearly dropped him.'

'Everything OK, kids?' Dad called. 'Do you want any help?'

'No!' shouted Oscar and Lucy at the same time.

'Phew!' Oscar said, as they staggered into Lucy's bedroom and gently lay Starlight, in his bundle, on to the soft bed. He was very calm and sweet. They made a little nest for him with Lucy's pillows, and Rocky and Scruffy looked on. Oscar and Lucy looked at each other and laughed as Starlight wriggled around, making himself comfortable.

'He's amazing,' Oscar said. Starlight snuffled and butted his head against Oscar's arm, lifting up his chin as if asking to be stroked. He was looking livelier already, and his fur was even

beginning to sparkle, although he didn't seem keen to get up and walk.

'I don't mind about getting presents any more—not even a kitten. I just want Starlight to get better,' Lucy said, anxiously. 'Do you think he'll be well enough to help Santa tomorrow?' she asked Oscar. They looked down at Starlight and he looked back and gave a little bleat.

They could hardly bear to leave Starlight to go down to dinner. Luckily, Dad and Mum were enjoying being together so much and were so busy chatting that they didn't notice Lucy and Oscar were never in the room at the same time.

'Can I say goodnight downstairs tonight?' Lucy asked at bedtime. 'I've got a special Christmas surprise in my room and I don't want you to see it.'

Mum and Dad laughed.

'OK, Lucy, we'll give you a hug down here then,' Dad said.

'I'm looking forward to this Christmas surprise!' Mum said, giving Lucy a kiss. 'Is it that puppet show you're making?'

'Not exactly,' Lucy said. 'Well, sort of. It's definitely Christmassy,' she added and rushed upstairs before they asked her any more questions.

Chapter Seven

Oscar came to give Starlight a last hug before he went to his room.

'Oscar, can you help me make the puppet show tomorrow?' Lucy asked. 'I've got to cuddle Starlight.'

'OK,' Oscar said. 'You're so lucky,'

he sighed. 'I wish he was in my room. See you tomorrow, Starlight.'

Lucy tried to get comfortable. It was definitely not easy sharing a bed with a little wriggly reindeer, no matter how soft and small he was. Finally, she decided to sit up, propped against her pillows. She would try to get him to settle down on her lap and go to sleep with his head resting on her arm.

'I'm going to hug you all night to get you better for tomorrow,' Lucy said, before quickly falling fast asleep herself.

Lucy woke to the sound of sleigh bells jingling. Moonlight was streaming into her room where Starlight had pushed the curtains apart. He was standing on the bed, wide awake and bleating excitedly. His two front hooves were on the windowsill, and his little tail was wagging madly. His fur was gleaming white, his nose black and shiny. He looked completely well!

Lucy got out of bed, opened the curtains properly, and looked out of the window. She had to rub her eyes to check whether she was dreaming. There, in the night sky, was Santa! He was dressed all in red and was sitting in a beautiful silver sleigh, pulled by nine big brown reindeer. The reindeer snorted and stamped their hooves in the air, their breath forming lightly sparkling clouds.

'Thank you, Lucy!' Santa called above the sound of sleigh bells. 'Starlight looks much better already!'

'What's going on?' came Oscar's sleepy voice. He was standing in the room, rubbing his eyes too. 'I heard the sleigh bells and Starlight bleating, so I came to see what was happening.'

Lucy pointed to the window, her mouth open in disbelief.

'Santa?' Oscar said in amazement.

'I can't believe it! You're in your sleigh and everything!'

Santa threw back his head and laughed, making Lucy and Oscar want to laugh too. 'Yes, Oscar—I am! How about you and Lucy come for a ride?' Santa said. 'Close your eyes and hold on to Starlight.'

Lucy and Oscar put their hands on Starlight and closed their eyes tight. Suddenly they felt tingly and fizzy and bubbly with happiness. Something wonderful was happening! Before they knew it, sleigh bells tinkled again and they found themselves outside, sitting next to Santa in his sleigh up in the sky.

Little Starlight was on his knee, sitting up, bright and alert.

'Wow! This is AMAZING!' laughed Oscar, hugging Lucy in his excitement.

'I can't believe it!' Lucy said, looking over the edge of the sleigh, down at the garden and the shed. Normally, Lucy would have been frightened to be up so high, but being in Santa's sleigh felt like the safest and happiest place in the whole world.

'Take this blanket and keep warm,' Santa said, tucking the blanket around their knees. His long white beard tickled Lucy as he leaned over. His red coat was soft and warm, and he smelled of cinnamon.

Starlight pointed his nose into the air, and the buds of his antlers began to glow, so that a tiny sparkling star appeared at the end of each one.

'Good boy, Starlight!' Santa laughed. 'Now we won't get lost! Hold on tight, you two!' And he twitched the reins signalling to the reindeer to start flying.

Off they went, through the night sky, swooping over seas and cities and mountains, flying past the moon almost touching the stars, and seeing their shadows fall on the fields below. They were as fast as the wind, but with Santa beside them they didn't feel scared at all.

'We're just practising for tomorrow!' Santa laughed, as they looked down on church steeples and forests, vast lakes, and busy cities twinkling with lights. 'So many children waiting for their presents—we mustn't get it wrong!' he said, as they flew over castles and cottages in the countryside, and blocks of flats and rows of houses in towns.

Starlight sparkled in the night, never losing his balance, his muzzle pointing into the wind and his little ears twitching with excitement. Santa would tell him a place to go and then one of the stars on his antler buds twinkled and flashed to tell Santa whether to turn left or right. When they went straight on, his little nose sparkled, too.

'He's a reindeer SatNav!' Oscar laughed. 'That's so cool!'

'So maybe when we see twinkling stars at night it's just Santa and Starlight planning their Christmas routes,' Lucy said.

'Exactly!' Santa laughed. 'We have to practise a lot to get it right for the big day. That's why Starlight is so important!'

It was all over too soon. Santa turned the sleigh around and they found themselves hovering in the air outside Lucy's room again. It seemed only minutes since the ride started, but they must have been out for much longer than that because the night sky was already getting lighter. It would soon be dawn.

'Well, this little fellow looks back to normal,' Santa said, giving Starlight a pat. 'He can't cope without his cuddles, and the elves have been so busy he has been fading away. I didn't think that he'd be ready for Christmas. But I knew you'd be able to make him better. I've got your Christmas letter safe and sound, by the way. Glad to see you wrote one in the end, Oscar!' Santa smiled at Oscar, his eyes twinkling.

Oscar blushed.

'And thanks for helping with Starlight. Christmas wouldn't be Christmas without my littlest reindeer. He points the way through the stars and finds the good in everyone.'

Lucy looked at Oscar. He was smiling at Santa and stroking Starlight's head. It was true. Starlight and Santa saw that Oscar was still kind, deep down, even if he could be the grumpiest brother in the world at times.

'We'll say goodbye, now,' Santa said. 'We have a busy time ahead. It's dawn here but we still have the other side of the world to visit!'

Lucy flung her arms around Starlight. He gave her a loving lick.

'I don't want to leave him!' cried Lucy, but the next thing she knew, she was waking up in her bed. Scruffy was next to her, and Rocky was looking over at her with his kind eyes. But there was no little reindeer.

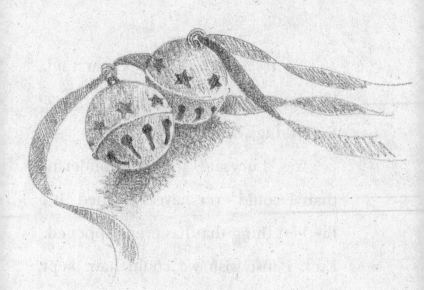

Chapter Eight

Lucy ran out of her bedroom and met Oscar on the landing. They looked at each other.

'Did you have a dream about—' they both said at the same time, and then stopped.

'So it *was* true then,' Oscar said. 'Starlight and the sleigh and Santa. Everything! Wow.'

'Yes,' Lucy said. 'It's more wonderful than I could ever have imagined. It's the best thing that has ever happened. Ever. I just wish we could have kept Starlight here. He's so sweet.'

'He'll be happier with Santa,' Oscar said. 'And Santa needs him—imagine all the children who wouldn't get presents if Starlight didn't guide the sleigh to their homes. Come on, Lucy, cheer up! Race you down to breakfast.'

'Who wants pancakes?' Dad asked cheerfully as they came into the kitchen. 'I've got a feeling this is going to be one of our best Christmases yet!' he said, getting out the frying pan.

Then his mobile phone rang.

'It's work,' he said, surprised. 'What are they doing, ringing me on Christmas Eve?' He picked it up, and then his face became very serious.

'Yes. Hello. Yes, I can talk now. Wait a minute, I'll take the phone into the next room.'

'Carry on without me,' he mouthed to Mum, and walked out of the kitchen.

Lucy and Oscar looked at each other. Why was Dad's work ringing him at Christmas?

They didn't have long to wait. Dad came back into the kitchen, a huge smile on his face. He went over to Mum and gave her a big hug, picking her up and whirling her round.

'You'll never guess! You remember I applied for that manager's job? More money and based locally? They have just rung to tell me I've got it! I start in the New Year! I won't have to travel away from home anymore!'

'I can't believe it!' Mum said. 'That's wonderful news!'

Everyone was so happy they didn't notice Lucy slipping away upstairs.

'I'm really glad Dad has a new job and we can all be together again,' she said to Scruffy and Rocky. 'But I miss Starlight so much. It's all I can think about. It was so special looking after him.'

There was a knock on the door.

'Are you OK, Lucy?' Mum asked.

'Yes, just a bit tired, that's all,' Lucy replied.

'Well, Dad says he wants to take us all out for lunch to celebrate, and then this afternoon I thought we could finish decorating the tree and maybe cuddle up and watch a film together? Dad and Gran and Oscar have to go out to do some special Christmas shopping now . . . Oh, I'm so happy, Lucy! I can't believe we're going to have Dad around at home again!' Mum gave Lucy a big hug, and Lucy could hear her singing as she went back downstairs.

'Thank you, Santa, for asking me to help make Starlight better,' Lucy said, once she was on her own. 'I'm sorry I'm not more happy. I will try.' She cuddled Scruffy and tried to be brave. Rocky seemed to rock a little, as if to say he understood.

'At least I have you two,' Lucy sighed.

The rest of the day was so busy that even though Lucy still had an ache inside from missing Starlight, she didn't really have time to be too sad. After a lovely lunch they came home to get on with getting ready for Christmas Day. Decorating the Christmas tree was always one of Lucy's favourite things to do. It was fun to find the Christmas fairy and put her back on top of the tree, and Dad and Mum kept talking about the new job.

Then the packages started appearing at the bottom of the tree. Gran came over with lots, including

a huge flat one and two smaller ones for Lucy. Upstairs, Lucy wrapped up a jewelry box she had made for Mum, a mug she had painted with 'Best Dad Ever!' on for Dad, a brooch with a badger on it for Gran, and a book of jokes for Oscar.

Before long, it was dark. They all wrapped up warm and went to hear the Christmas carols in town. They ate hot chestnuts as the brass band played. Little flakes of snow drifted down and the lights in the shop fronts twinkled. It was magical.

'This is the best Christmas ever!' Oscar said.

If only we still had Starlight, Lucy thought, but she didn't say anything.

Chapter Nine

Lucy woke up to the sound of loud drumming.

'Put the headphones on, Oscar!' Dad shouted, but he didn't sound too cross.

Remembering that it was Christmas Day, Lucy quickly opened her eyes. Her stocking at the end of the bed was bulging! There was a long shape wrapped in colourful paper poking out of the top, and when she held the toe of the stocking, she could feel lots of hard little flat round shapes. Chocolate coins! And a new red pencil case with her name on it in gold swirly letters! Inside the case there were beautiful coloured pens with her name in gold on each of them, too. Lucy ate two chocolate coins and smiled as she thought of how Starlight must've been well enough to guide Santa to her house in the night.

She tried not to be sad that he hadn't been able to stay and see her open her presents.

Oscar was eventually persuaded off the drums and they all had a special Christmas breakfast together. There were scrambled eggs and thick slices of warm, buttered toast, and Mum had made freshly squeezed orange juice. Mum was really happy with the decorated box Lucy had made for her, and Dad loved his painted mug.

'I'll have my Christmas cuppa in it!' Dad said, beaming.

'Thank you so much, Lucy!' Mum said. 'What a lovely surprise! No wonder you were so mysterious and busy yesterday!' Lucy squirmed a little, and didn't say that she had made the gifts at school.

Lucy was given a smart new watch from Mum and Dad, and a false moustache set from Oscar. They were all trying on moustaches and laughing when the doorbell rang. Mum and Dad looked at each other and smiled.

'Go and answer that, Lucy,' Dad said.

Excited, Lucy went to open the door.

'Hello, Lucy! Happy Christmas, darling!' Gran said, hugging her with one arm because the other was holding a big wicker basket.

When Gran and Lucy came into the sitting room Oscar and Dad and Mum were standing in front of the Christmas tree, smiling.

'Have you given it to her yet?' Oscar asked Gran.

'No,' Gran said, laughing. She passed the basket to Dad, who carefully put it down.

'Lucy, come and open the lid,' said Mum. 'Whatever is inside is for you!'

Lucy opened it and looked inside. There was something small and ginger and furry—she couldn't believe it! Carefully she reached inside and brought out . . . a tiny little kitten! It had big blue eyes, a little pink nose, and soft fluffy fur.

'Oh!' Lucy said. 'She's beautiful!'

'She's yours,' Dad said. 'Because you are such a kind girl. We can't think of anyone better to look after her.' Lucy couldn't stop smiling. Santa had made her wish come true!

The rest of Christmas Day was the happiest day Lucy could remember. Mum and Dad made a delicious Christmas lunch with all the trimmings. Oscar (with his headphones on) played the drums, and Gran and Lucy played with the little kitten. At first she was shy, and cuddled up on Lucy's lap, watching everyone with her big kitten eyes. But soon she began to explore, and then decided that Christmas was the most fun ever. She chased ribbons and even tried to climb the tree! After lunch, she jumped on the Christmas paper as Lucy unwrapped the big flat package from Gran.

'It's a puppet theatre! Thanks, Gran!' Lucy said. 'You can have your velvet curtain back, Mum. I didn't have time to use it to make my own theatre, and now I don't need it. Look what Gran got me!'

It was beautiful—painted red and gold and made of three sections which stood up when unfolded with a red velvet curtain for the background. But the puppets were even better. They were beautifully painted wooden stick puppets—one of Santa and his silver sleigh being pulled by nine reindeer, and then one tiny little reindeer puppet on its own.

'How unusual!' Mum said, admiring them. 'Wherever did you get them?' she asked Gran.

'From a very special workshop,' Gran replied, and smiled at Oscar and Lucy. 'This little reindeer is very sweet. I wonder what his name is. It can't be Rudolph because there's already one with a red nose pulling the sleigh.'

'It's Starlight,' Lucy said, looking down at the little puppet, and she and Oscar smiled at each other. They knew exactly what their puppet show would be about.

'And what are you going to call this little one?' Mum asked.

The kitten jumped off Lucy's lap and rushed around the room, pouncing on stray bits of Christmas paper and leaping up on to the drums and down again. Everyone laughed. She was a totally gorgeous, completely mad ball of fluff.

'Merry!' Lucy said. 'Because this really is a merry Christmas!'

At the end of what had been a very happy Christmas Day, Oscar reluctantly left his drum kit and went to bed with his joke book, and Gran went home to feed the animals. Merry the kitten had played herself to sleep, curled up next to Scruffy, warm and snug on Lucy's bed.

'I can't believe you're here,' Lucy marvelled, stroking her sleepily. It was certainly easier to cuddle a kitten than a reindeer. 'Thank you, Santa. I hope Starlight isn't too tired after his big day.'

Soon after, Mum and Dad came to kiss her goodnight.

'Sleep well, Lucy. Sleep well, Merry.' Mum laughed as the kitten stretched out her little legs. She looked as happy and relaxed as Mum and Dad did. 'I loved your puppet show about the reindeer Starlight who needed to get well for Christmas,' Mum said.

'Sweet dreams, lovely Lucy,' Dad said, as he kissed her. 'It's been a great Christmas, hasn't it? All our wishes have come true!' He blew her another kiss as he pulled the door closed behind them.

'Goodnight, Rocky, goodnight, Scruffy, goodnight, Merry,' Lucy said. She looked at the softly-glowing night light

beside her bed, with the snowflakes falling on the little house. For a moment, she thought the door of the house opened and a small figure, dressed in red, came out, with a tiny white deer running excitedly around in circles at his feet. He looked up at her and waved. She rubbed her eyes and looked again, but if there had been

anything there, it was gone. No Santa, no reindeer, just snow falling on a little house in the woods. Yet Lucy smiled as she remembered the sleigh ride, and the softness of Starlight's fur, and how Santa had smelled of cinnamon.

'Goodnight Santa, goodnight Starlight—wherever you both are! Happy Christmas, and thank you!' Lucy whispered. And, kissing Merry on top of her warm little head, Lucy settled down to go to sleep.

LUCY'S MAGIC
SNOW GLOBE

Written by
Anne Booth

Illustrated by
Sophy Williams

OXFORD
UNIVERSITY PRESS

To my dear friends Katy, Simon,
Lizzie, and Esther Burder

Chapter One

21st December

It was Christmas time and Lucy's home was full of delicious baking smells, fairy lights, and decorations. It was especially busy in Lucy's house this year because her dad's friends from Australia were coming to stay with them for Christmas.

They were supposed to be moving in to a house in the village, but their new home wouldn't be ready until the New Year.

Lucy was in her bedroom with her little cat Merry, her pyjama-case dog Scruffy, and her rocking horse, Rocky.

She was sitting cross-legged on her bed, shaking her snow globe. She loved the snow globe. It lit up at night and there was a pretty Christmassy woodland scene inside. Once, she had even thought she'd seen Father Christmas and a reindeer. It normally cheered her up to watch the pretty white and silver flakes falling, but today she sighed.

'Christmas was going to be really special this year. Gran was coming to stay in my room after her shoulder operation and now it's all changed. It was going to be like a fun sleepover with Gran, but now Mum says I have to sleep downstairs with this girl called Sita . . .' said Lucy to her three friends. 'I've never even met her and I've got to share a room with her just because she's the same age as me. What if she doesn't like animals? What if she doesn't like naughty cats like you, Merry?'

Lucy put the snow globe carefully back on her windowsill and rolled a pen across the room for Merry, who jumped on it delightedly. She never tired of that game.

'Lucy? Have you cleared your bedroom yet?' called Mum up the stairs. Lucy looked at the floor. It had been fine before Merry had padded upstairs to pay her a visit. First Merry had jumped on the wastepaper basket and tipped all the rubbish out. She had looked so sweet patting all the scrunched-up paper and chasing old pens that Lucy had forgotten that she was supposed to be getting her room ready for Gran. Then Merry had jumped up on the chest of drawers and knocked a pot of glitter all over Lucy's bedroom carpet.

'Oh, Merry! You really are a Christmas cat now!' Lucy had laughed, as Merry left little glittery paw prints all over the room. 'It's a good thing I've made all the Christmas cards already.'

This year Lucy had made lots of Christmas cards and drawn a picture of a special magic baby reindeer on the front of each, so she had needed lots of glitter. She had sold them on a stall at school to raise money for her gran's Wildlife Rescue Centre. Then she gave the money and a special card on which she had written 'Get Well Soon' to Gran in the hospital. Gran had put it beside her hospital bed.

'Oh, Lucy!' Gran had said. 'This is definitely the nicest card in the ward! What a kind girl you are! I can't wait until Christmas. We'll have a special girls' sleepover, you and me, and talk about what we'll do when the Wildlife Rescue Centre opens again. At least whilst I'm in hospital I can make the Centre better. I'm getting so much building work done and it would have been too noisy for the sick animals if they'd been there. We're having a bigger kitchen with new sinks and cupboards, and a little quiet area, and even a new aviary at the back. There are going to be heated cages and a place for bigger animals in the garden too. It'll be wonderful. So it's all worked out very well, and we're so lucky that Meadowbank Sanctuary took the little hedgehogs and the robin.'

It was really exciting but Lucy missed Gran and helping out at the Centre very much. But she was glad that the operation was over and that Gran was coming to stay for a few weeks. Lucy had planned to spend their sleepover time every day talking about how they would look after the hedgehogs and deer and foxes and owls and other birds and animals when the Centre opened again. Lucy loved animals so much.

'Oh, Lucy!' Mum was in the doorway looking hot and bothered. She was holding one end of a camp bed she had got out of the attic, and Oscar, Lucy's big brother, who was in his first year at secondary school, was holding the other. 'This room was supposed to be ready by now. Honestly, Lucy—what a mess!'

'I'm sorry, Mum,' said Lucy, trying to ignore the pretend-shocked face Oscar was pulling behind Mum's back. He could be so annoying. And he didn't even have to move out of his bedroom. It wasn't fair. 'It was ready but Merry tipped the wastepaper basket over.'

'Well, she'll have to go downstairs in her basket for now. I'm not even sure if she should sleep on your bed in the kitchen whilst our visitors are here, Lucy,' said Mum. 'Go downstairs and put her in the sitting room and then come back up and sort out this room with me.'

Lucy scooped Merry up from the floor into her arms. Even though Mum was cross, she couldn't help smiling at the naughty little cat. Ever since she had arrived in their home as a little Christmas kitten, the whole family loved her, but Lucy loved her most of all, and one of her favourite things in

the world was going to sleep with Merry
curled up beside Scruffy, her pyjama-
case dog, with Rocky the rocking horse
looking on with his kind, patient eyes.

Mum and Oscar opened out the
camp bed in Lucy's room for Lucy's
sleepover night with Gran. When the
visitors arrived, both girls would sleep

on camp beds in the kitchen, and Dad and Mum were going to be sleeping in the lounge and giving their bed to Sita's parents. 'It's not fair if you can't sleep on my bed just because that girl is coming,' grumbled Lucy to Merry as she put her down in her basket in the sitting room. Merry was perfectly happy there and curled up to go to sleep, but Lucy still felt cross as she went back upstairs. The house was full of sparkly decorations and the Christmas tree was up, but Lucy didn't feel Christmassy any more at all.

'Why do we have to have visitors?' she muttered as she tidied up.

'I think we're going to have to put Rocky in the garage over Christmas,' said Mum, looking around Lucy's room. 'Some of the luggage from Australia can go in Oscar's room, but we'll have to store some in your room too. Gran says she doesn't mind.'

'No! It's not fair!' said Lucy, shocked. 'Poor Rocky! He hasn't done anything wrong. He'll want to stay with Gran or me. He'll be so lonely in the garage. Please, Mum—don't put him there!'

'Oh, Lucy,' sighed Mum. She called Oscar into Lucy's room. 'Look—why don't you two go out to the park? I'll try to sort the rooms out and make things fit.'

'Do I have to take Lucy with me?' complained Oscar. 'My friends will probably be there having a kick-around, and she'll just get in the way.'

'Yes, you do,' said Mum. 'You both need some fresh air and I need some space. Take your phone, Oscar.'

The weather was very cold and damp, and Oscar and Lucy both put their coats on very grumpily.

'Hurry up, Lucy!' Oscar said, and ran ahead. Lucy had to run her fastest to catch up with him.

'Hi, Will!' Oscar shouted when he saw his friends. He rushed over to them.

Lucy felt cross and tired and left out. She didn't feel like playing on the slide and the swings on her own. She would much rather have been at home with Merry and Rocky and Scruffy. She sat on the bench and thought about her best school friend.

'I can't even visit Rosie because her family have gone to her Grandad's for Christmas,' she sighed.

Lucy got up and walked around the edge of the football pitch. Suddenly, she noticed something moving in the hedge. She bent down and moved the branches to one side and there, on the cold ground, was a tiny baby rabbit, all alone and with a nasty cut on his leg. He was very sweet but Lucy knew he was also very poorly. He didn't try to run away when he saw her. Instead, he just lay there with his ears back, looking frightened.

'Oh, please don't be scared,' whispered Lucy. She knew from her work with her

gran that you shouldn't normally
touch a wild animal, but she could
see that this little rabbit was injured.

She looked around but there was no sign of rabbit holes or any warren for it to shelter in, just a flat football pitch beside a road. He wouldn't survive on his own. He really needed her help.

Chapter Two

'Oscar!' Lucy called, but he was busy with his friends.

'Over here, Sam!' Oscar shouted, as he ran to receive the ball.

'Oscar!' Lucy yelled again, but it was no use. Lucy summoned up all her courage and ran onto the field to get him.

'Hey, Oscar! Your sister's on the pitch!' the other footballers complained. Lucy wanted to run off, but she knew the baby rabbit was depending on her to get help.

'What are you doing?' Oscar said, annoyed, as he ran over.

'Oscar—look what I've found in the bushes. It's a little rabbit and he's hurt,' said Lucy, leading Oscar to the hedge. Oscar's best friends Will and Fergus left the others and came over to see.

'Where has he come from?' said Oscar, kneeling down.

'I don't know but we can't leave him here. He won't survive now he's hurt. I'm going to have to bring him home. He needs to be kept warm,' said Lucy, unzipping her coat.

'You can have my old jumper if you like—I was using it as one of the goalposts,' said Fergus, and he ran to get it.

Lucy gently placed Fergus's jumper over the rabbit and scooped it up so that the rabbit was cosy and securely wrapped, and couldn't kick. Then she carried it inside her coat. She could feel his heart thumping against her chest.

'Don't worry, little rabbit,' she whispered to it. 'I'll be your friend. I will look after you.'

Oscar, Will, and Fergus walked back with Lucy, past the houses with all the Christmas decorations in their gardens and windows. Will and Fergus didn't normally talk to her. It felt good being in a group of friends for a little while, even if they were big boys.

'Will your sister be able to help it?' she heard Will ask Oscar.

'Yeah—she does lots with my gran so she knows loads about animals. She'll be able to make it better,' said Oscar confidently.

Lucy felt really proud. Oscar didn't often say nice things about her. Most of the time he was too busy at school or playing football or drums to really notice her. She didn't mind too much as she was mostly with Gran, helping out at the Centre, or playing with Merry, or visiting Rosie in the next village, but it felt good to hear him say that to his friends. Maybe they would talk to her more now.

'Mum—Lucy's back with a rabbit!' called Oscar up the stairs when they got back. 'Fergus and Will and I are going back down the park. Bye!' and the boys banged the door behind them and ran off back to their game, leaving Lucy on her own in the hallway, holding her warm bundle.

'Lucy?' said Mum, coming out on to the landing. 'What's that you've got?'

'It's a little rabbit, Mum. It was injured and I couldn't leave it under the hedge alone,' said Lucy.

'Oh, dear,' Mum sighed, her arms full of sheets. 'What are we going to do? I suppose we could take it to the big wildlife sanctuary, but that means a two-hour round trip, and I've got so much to do. Is it very badly hurt?'

'I'm not sure. He has a cut on his leg, and he's so small and away from his warren. He won't survive on his own. Can't I look after him—please?' pleaded Lucy. 'I've helped Gran with baby rabbits before. I know where she keeps her special baby rabbit food.'

Just then they heard the key in the lock and Dad came in, looking very cheerful and wearing some tinsel around his head.

'I'm on holiday—hooray! Christmas starts NOW!' he said, and went to give Lucy a hug.

'No, Dad—I've got a baby rabbit in my coat,' said Lucy.

'Have you, indeed?' said Dad. 'Can I have a look?'

Mum came down the stairs and they all peeped in. The tiny rabbit's eyes were closed, and it was breathing very fast.

'He's very sweet, but he looks poorly, Lucy,' said Mum.

'I don't think we should drive it miles away to the wildlife sanctuary. I think it needs peace and quiet to get better,' said Lucy. 'Please, Dad— please can we get one of Gran's cages and the baby rabbit food and bring it here tonight? I do know what to do, honestly.'

Dad looked at Mum.

'Just for tonight, Lucy,' said Mum.

'Your dad or I will have to take it to the wildlife sanctuary tomorrow as we just won't have room when our visitors come.'

Lucy opened her mouth to argue but her dad gave her a wink.

'Come on Lucy Lu—pop the little fellow in Merry's cat basket for five minutes and we'll drive to Gran's quickly and collect the stuff you need.'

Merry rushed out into the hallway as if she heard her name.

'Now, Merry, we're borrowing your cat carrier,' said Lucy. 'This baby rabbit is called a kitten, like you were, and he needs quiet, like Gran does, to get better.' Lucy got the wicker cat carrier from the hall cupboard and moved some Christmas cards to the side to make room for it on the hall table. Lucy carefully laid the little rabbit in Fergus's old jumper inside the carrier and closed the door. Then she picked up Merry and gave her a quick cuddle and kiss on the top of her head. The little cat purred and didn't want to be put down.

'I'm sorry, Merry, but I'm going to lock you in the kitchen. I don't trust you not to bother the kitten,' said Lucy. Merry gave an indignant mew and they could hear her scratching at the door as they left.

'Your gran will be very proud of you,' said Lucy's dad in Gran's house. They packed some rabbit food and some hay in a cage, ready to bring home. 'But Lucy, I think your Mum is right—I'm not sure we can look after it over Christmas with all our visitors here too.'

'I wish they weren't coming,' said Lucy. 'There isn't enough room, and they are just making things difficult.'

'Don't say that, Lucy,' said Dad. 'I want you to make Sita, and her dad and mum welcome. It's not easy for them being away from the rest of their family at Christmas. They need friends.'

'Why did they come then?' said Lucy.

'Sita's dad, Prajit, is coming to work here for a year. Sita is going to your school, so that's why I want you to be friends. It'll be too busy at our house for you to look after this little chap—you'll need to take care of Sita.'

'I'd rather look after the rabbit,' said Lucy.

'I'm sure that's true, Lucy,' said Dad, smiling, 'but poor Sita needs a friend too!'

When they got home, Lucy rushed to the hall table and looked inside the carrier to see how the rabbit was. He was very weak when they took him out of Merry's cat basket, and he didn't try

to struggle whilst Dad helped to hold him and Lucy bathed his leg as Gran had taught her. Then they transferred him to the cage. Oscar came back from football and they all sat down to dinner. Merry crept in and sat on Lucy's feet like an extra furry slipper.

The phone rang just as they were clearing the table. Mum went to answer it and came back smiling.

'Well, it's good news from the hospital. They say Gran can leave the ward and we can go and collect her straight away,' she said.

'Hooray!' said Lucy. 'I can ask her about the rabbit.'

'I just don't know how we are going to fit everyone in!' said Mum to Dad.

'We'll manage!' said Dad, giving her a hug. 'Come on, Lucy—let's go and get her now!'

Chapter Three

'Well done, Lucy!' said Gran. She gave the little rabbit a very quick examination. 'You've done just the right thing. It's a little male rabbit. He would never have managed on his own with a hurt paw like that.'

'Couldn't we just find a rabbit burrow and leave him there?' said Oscar.

'No, I'm afraid that would be very dangerous. You can't put a wild rabbit down any old burrow. We don't know where he comes from, and the rabbits already in the burrow might think he was an enemy and fight him. He would have no warren to live in and have to live above ground on his own—and that isn't safe. He's not ready to go anywhere yet anyway—he is far too weak.'

Gran settled in the armchair next to the Christmas tree. Merry was curled up on her lap, purring loudly. 'I'm so looking forward to the work being finished on the Centre, and planning next year.'

Lucy really did want to talk about the Centre with Gran, but first of all she wanted to talk about the little rabbit.

'Gran, I know the visitors haven't come yet—but would you mind if I slept downstairs tonight too so I can keep an eye on him?' said Lucy. 'I can sleep in the kitchen with Rocky and Scruffy. I can't sleep upstairs knowing that he is downstairs all alone, with no friends.'

'I think that's a lovely idea,' said Gran, smiling at her.

It was fun getting ready to sleep in the kitchen. Dad agreed to bring Rocky down, and Lucy brought Scruffy down too.

'We're having a sleepover with a rabbit,' she whispered in his ear.

Mum and Dad brought the camp

bed down and made it very warm and cosy, and Mum even put a hot-water bottle in it. Merry kept on getting in everyone's way, hiding under the pillows and burrowing under the duvet to find the hot-water bottle.

Lucy went upstairs to kiss Gran goodnight.

'If only we could find the rabbit's family,' said Lucy. 'It seems so sad not to be with your family at Christmas.'

'I'll help you look after him, Lucy,' said Gran. 'We might have to take him over to the wildlife sanctuary and see if we can gradually introduce him to a new warren in a safe area. It's not easy. It takes a lot of time, and the wild rabbits have to be allowed to come and sniff him through the wire fence so that they accept him.'

'What if they don't accept him?' said Lucy.

'Well, then we'd have to keep him in the Centre because it would be too dangerous for him on his own.'

'Come on, Lucy,' called Mum. 'Time for bed! Kiss Gran goodnight and come downstairs.'

Mum had brought in a coffee table and a little reading lamp, and Lucy put her snow globe on the table beside her.

'Goodnight, Lucy. Sleep well,' said

Mum, and she gave Lucy a hug. 'Have some hot chocolate and read a little bit of your book, and then go and brush your teeth. We'll come and kiss you goodnight on our way to bed.'

The kitchen seemed different after bedtime. Mum switched off the lights but left the one over the cooker on. Lucy had to remind herself that the shadows on the back of the door were only Mum and Dad's aprons hanging on the peg, the dark shapes in the corner were only Oscar's football boots, and the shapes coming down from the ceiling were only the pots and pans hanging from the rack. Outside the kitchen window, the garden seemed dark and mysterious. Inside, the fridge shivered and the ticking of the kitchen clock sounded much louder than during the day, but with Merry and Scruffy and Rocky, Lucy felt fine. It was a fun adventure to be sleeping somewhere new with friends—even if it was just the kitchen!

'Don't be frightened,' she called over softly to the sleeping rabbit. 'If you wake in the night, we're all here with you.'

Lucy finished her hot chocolate and went upstairs to the bathroom.

On her way back downstairs from brushing her teeth, Lucy heard Mum and Dad talking in the sitting room.

'I'm not sure if I can cope with a sick rabbit as well as Christmas for four more people,' said Mum.

'Don't worry,' said Dad. 'Lucy and I will take it to the sanctuary tomorrow.'

'It isn't fair,' said Lucy crossly as she got into bed. Merry was already curled up next to Scruffy on top of the duvet. Lucy looked over at Rocky and then at the cage. 'I hope he is going to be all right,' she said. The little rabbit stirred.

Lucy switched her reading lamp off but switched the snow globe on so that it lit up. She picked it up and shook the globe so the snow fell on the cottage inside.

'I wish you were a magic snow globe,' said Lucy. 'I'd close my eyes like this . . .' She closed her eyes as tight as she could and felt the cool globe in her hands. '. . . And I'd say, "I wish for that little rabbit to get better; I wish he could be back with his family for Christmas; and I wish for Christmas to be like it always is." '

All at once, Lucy felt her hands tingle. She opened her eyes quickly and saw that the globe was glowing brighter and brighter, the sparkling silver and white snowflakes falling faster and faster, even though she wasn't shaking the globe any more. Suddenly, Lucy was sure that beyond the twirling snowflakes she could see a tiny figure of Father Christmas outside the little house in the woods. He was waving to her and holding a sweet baby reindeer in his arms. At the same time, she heard the sound of sleigh bells and the globe felt warm in her hands. Then the whirling white and silver snowflakes were joined by first green and then red ones, and then all the snowflakes became tiny glittering stars of all the colours of the rainbow, filling the globe.

'You ARE a magic snow globe!' said Lucy in delight. Her heart beat fast with excitement and she felt a wave of

happiness from the top of her head to the tips of her toes.

Lucy blinked hard and shook her head, but when she looked back there was no snow falling, no rainbow stars, no Father Christmas, or baby reindeer. The tingling stopped and the snow globe felt cool as she held it. Everything was back to normal—it was just a pretty snow globe with a tiny house in a still wood with snow lying peacefully on the ground—but inside Lucy still felt fizzy with happiness.

'What just happened?' said Lucy out loud to Rocky, Merry, and Scruffy. 'Did I dream that?' Merry gave a little mew. She put her paws on Lucy's chest and climbed up, touching her little pink nose to Lucy's and looking into Lucy's eyes. Then she jumped onto Lucy's pillow and curled herself up, purring so much that Lucy could feel the vibrations.

'Merry! I don't speak "purr"! And you're so loud!' laughed Lucy. 'How am I going to sleep if you purr like that? I still don't know if the globe is really magic or if I only dreamt it. But I'm suddenly so, so tired. I think I'll just lie down next to you and . . .'

When Lucy's parents tiptoed in, only the light above the cooker and the light from the snow globe were on. Lucy was fast asleep, holding Scruffy, with Merry beside her and Rocky standing guard. They kissed her goodnight, and, as they closed the door and Lucy and Merry and the little rabbit stirred and slept, the pretty silver and white snowflakes inside the globe began to fall again, even though Lucy had not shaken it.

Chapter Four

22nd December

The rabbit was still sleeping when Lucy woke the next morning to the sound of Dad filling the kettle and whistling Christmas carols. Merry was also asleep on the pillow next to her. Lucy stroked her and she stretched and purred but didn't wake up. The snow globe was on the table. No snow was falling. It all looked completely normal.

'It must have all been just a lovely dream,' said Lucy, giving Scruffy a hug.

Lucy got out of bed and put on her dressing gown and slippers. First she went to check on the rabbit, but he didn't want to eat any of the food she tried to give him. He just lay with his eyes closed, his soft furry body going up and down with his breathing.

'Morning, Lucy Lu!' said Dad, giving her a kiss. 'I'm going to take your gran and your mum a cup of tea in bed. Do you want to help me?'

Lucy carefully carried a cup up to Gran.

'Thank you, Lucy,' said Gran. 'How is the rabbit?'

'He's not really eating yet,' said Lucy. 'He's sleeping.'

Gran took a sip of her tea. 'Poor little chap. Maybe he needs some more rest. It must have been a shock for him. I've got to do what the doctor said and have a little rest this morning too, but I'll come down later and we'll check him out. Don't worry.'

'Now, Lucy, I'll fold up the bed,' said Dad, when Lucy came back down to the kitchen. 'Please can you put the coffee table and the lamp away?'

Lucy slipped the snow globe into her pocket and carried the little table and the lamp back into the sitting room. Dad had switched on the fairy lights already and it looked warm and cheery.

'Well done, Lucy!' said Dad when she returned to the kitchen. 'I'll put the pillows and duvet in a bag in this cupboard, ready for tonight.'

Lucy walked over to check on the tiny rabbit. He looked back at her, his eyes open and his nose twitching, but he wasn't interested in the food in his cage. His fur looked so soft and brown, she longed to pick him up and give him a hug, but she knew from Gran that wild animals don't enjoy being cuddled.

She put her hand in her pocket and felt the smooth roundness of the snow globe. 'I wished you'd be better and home for Christmas,' she whispered to the rabbit. She checked Dad wasn't looking—he was busy making room in the cupboard for the bedding—and took the snow globe out quickly. But it looked just like it always did—not magic in the least. She must have imagined it after all. Lucy felt a little disappointed.

She had so wanted to help the rabbit.

'Lucy—what's this?' asked Dad. 'I found it under your pillow.' He gave Lucy a little red cloth pouch as he took the folded-up bed out to the garage.

Lucy had never seen the red pouch before. It was as red as Father Christmas's coat, and it sparkled as Lucy held it. It was so beautiful, embroidered with a picture of Father Christmas and a little white Christmas reindeer. Lucy opened the pouch, and inside was glittering, magical dust—all the colours of the rainbow, just like the stars she had seen in the globe. Folded up small and covered in glitter was a note. Lucy felt her heart beating fast. Her fingers were tingling the way they had felt when she had wished on the snow globe—something magical was happening, she was sure of it. She opened the note and read:

To Lucy,

This magic dust is especially for you
For with your kind heart you will know what to do.
So sprinkle it carefully down from above
On those who are lost and need friendship and love
And magic will happen for them and for you
And your Christmas wishes will then all come true.

What could it mean? Lucy was puzzling over the note when Oscar came rushing into the kitchen. Lucy hastily put the note in her pocket.

'I'm late to meet Will and Fergus,' he said, picking up his football boots from the corner.

'I need you to come back and clear your room later, Oscar,' said Dad, coming back into the room. 'We're going to have to put some luggage in there.'

'But Dad—what about my drums and all my other stuff?' complained Oscar. He looked at the clock. 'OK, I'll do it later. I'm late! I'll be back for lunch!' and suddenly he was off, banging the door behind him.

'Hmm. I'll have to make sure he remembers,' said Dad. 'Right,' he said to Lucy. 'I've just put some washing in the machine. Your mum and I have to go and do some more Christmas shopping this morning. Our visitors should be arriving tonight. Will you be OK staying here downstairs on your own this morning? I think we should let Gran have a sleep.'

'That's fine, Dad!' said Lucy, trying not to look too excited. She couldn't wait until everyone had gone so she could look at the magic note again. She felt bubbly with happiness. Something amazing was happening, and she wanted to look at the note and the magic dust properly when nobody else was there.

Chapter Five

When her mum and dad had gone out, Lucy quickly got dressed. She felt so excited about the pouch. Merry made a bit of a fuss mewing for her breakfast, winding in and out of Lucy's legs, so Lucy fed her and then Merry disappeared through the cat flap.

Lucy quickly put her pyjamas back inside Scruffy so that he looked lovely and plump again. She put him on top of Rocky in the corner of the kitchen. 'I suppose you eat pyjamas for breakfast,' she said to Scruffy, as she poured some Krispies into her bowl and added the milk. Normally she loved to listen to the rice pop, but today she was too busy reading and rereading the note to pay much attention. The paper itself glowed and sparkled as if it was trying to help her understand the words.

Suddenly, the telephone rang. Maybe it was Mum or Dad checking on her, or asking what she would like for tea?

'Hello?' said Lucy.

'Hello, Lucy!' said a man's friendly voice. 'This is your dad's friend, Prajit. We managed to get an earlier flight and so we'll be with you in about five minutes. Is your dad there?'

'No,' said Lucy. 'He'll be back soon.'

'I'll ring him on his mobile then,' said Prajit. He had an Australian accent and sounded kind. 'We'll see you very soon! Bye!'

Lucy put the phone down.

'Oh no!' she said to Rocky and Scruffy. 'The visitors are coming any minute!'

She ran over to check on the rabbit, but he was still asleep. She put the note back in the red pouch with the glitter, and carefully put it in her pocket. Then she washed up her cereal bowl and spoon, and put the cereal box back in the cupboard so that the kitchen table was tidy.

She heard the key turn in the door, and her mum and dad rushed back in.

'We've just spoken to Prajit so we came straight back!' said Mum. 'The rooms aren't ready! What shall we do?'

At that moment the doorbell rang and the house was full of cheery voices and laughter and people hugging.

Prajit and his wife Joanna were really friendly, and as soon as Mum saw them, she relaxed and started smiling. Sita, their daughter, was smaller than Lucy expected. She had big brown eyes like her dad and long dark hair. She was wearing a pretty blue velvet hairband with her name on it in silver. Lucy thought it was lovely. Sita wasn't smiley like her mum and dad. She hid behind her mum and wouldn't even look at Lucy.

'It's so lovely of you to have us for Christmas whilst we wait for the house to be ready!' said Joanna. 'We're so sorry to land ourselves on you like this.'

She handed Mum some parcels. 'We've brought some Christmas presents from Australia for you!'

At lunchtime, Dad went into the kitchen with Prajit to put the pizzas in the oven and catch up with his friend's news. Joanna and Sita stayed in the sitting room with Mum and Lucy. Oscar came back and went up to his room to get changed out of his football gear.

'Don't be silly, Sita. Say hello to Lucy,' said Joanna, but Sita just shook her head and looked down.

'I'm sorry, Lucy,' said Joanna. 'Sita's a bit tired from a long flight and she is missing her friends.'

'I'll just go and ask Gran if she wants any pizza,' said Lucy. She didn't want to have to stay in the sitting room with everyone, and especially Sita, who didn't seem to like her at all.

'Good girl!' said Mum. 'I'm sure she'll want to come down and join us.'

As Lucy went up the stairs, she could hear Joanna saying how lovely the Christmas decorations were and how exciting it would be if it snowed when they were in England. Sita didn't say anything at all.

Chapter Six

Gran came down, and everyone was very cheerful at lunch apart from Sita, who kept very quiet and wouldn't look at anyone.

'We need to pop into town to get some surprises,' said Joanna. 'We thought we'd do it before our journey catches up on us and we have to go to sleep. Is it OK if we leave Sita here with you?'

'Of course!' said Mum. 'Lucy and I were going to do our Christmas baking—it will be lovely to have her with us, won't it, Lucy?'

Lucy nodded, but she didn't want to say 'yes' out loud as it wasn't really true. She liked her special Christmas baking time with just her and Mum.

'That's lovely. Sita loves baking, don't you?' said Joanna, but Sita just put her arms around her mum and hid her head.

'Can I join in with the baking?' said Gran, which made Lucy feel a bit better.

'What about Oscar? Isn't he doing any baking? Come on—you can't just leave it to the girls!' said Prajit.

'And me? I think I'll do some too this year!' said Dad, looking over at Sita and giving her a wink. 'Perhaps Sita can give me some tips!'

After lunch, Joanna and Prajit went off to do their shopping. They said they would pick up the last bits of Christmas food Mum and Dad hadn't managed to get. Dad made Oscar stay and bake with everybody else. Oscar was a bit grumpy at first, and the kitchen felt a bit crowded, but Dad put on loud Christmas songs and gave everyone silly Christmas hats to wear. Lucy put hers on and went over to the side to see the rabbit. He had his eyes closed and was breathing heavily. He wasn't well.

'I'm sorry it's a bit noisy. It must be so awful feeling lost and ill away from your friends in the warren,' she whispered. Then she remembered:

. . . sprinkle it carefully down from above

On those who are lost and need friendship

and love . . .

'I think I know what to do!' Lucy said to herself. She checked nobody was watching and took the pouch out.

She nearly dropped it in surprise—the little figures of Father Christmas and the reindeer seemed to be moving! They looked like the figures she had seen in the snow globe. Father Christmas waved at her and the reindeer ran around in a circle.

They're telling me I've got it right! thought Lucy excitedly. *I've got to sprinkle it on the rabbit.*

'Come on, Lucy!' called Dad. 'We've got to make the cake mixture!'

'I'll be back as soon as I can,' whispered Lucy to the rabbit.

Although Lucy was impatient to be alone with the rabbit and use the magic dust, it was still fun cooking with Dad. Even Sita smiled a little when Dad showed everyone how to crack eggs and do a silly dance at the same time. Mum told him to stop but she kept laughing. They all did a silly dance around the kitchen, and then Dad asked Sita to show him how to put the cake mixture into the cases, and kept making deliberate mistakes to make her laugh.

Lucy beamed with excitement. She couldn't wait to see if she was right about the note. Dad saw her and laughed, and gave her a hug.

'We're going to have a great Christmas—I can feel it!' he said.

I know it, thought Lucy, touching the soft magical pouch in her pocket.

As soon as the cakes were in the oven and the others had all gone into the sitting room, Lucy took out the pouch.

'I think this dust might make you feel better,' she whispered to the rabbit. 'I made a wish on my snow globe and then this pouch arrived, so it must be magical,' and she quickly sprinkled some of the sparkling dust over the cage.

Lucy gasped as the wonderful sparkling dust didn't fall on the cage floor, but instead rose up in the air in a beautiful glittering rainbow cloud and whirled round and round the little rabbit. His eyes opened and he looked straight into hers. Lucy felt in her heart how much he wanted to go home, but she also felt certain that, somehow, the magic dust would help him.

'Everything is going to be all right—I just know it,' she whispered to him. He wriggled his nose and the magic dust disappeared, but Lucy felt sure everything was going to be fine.

'Hey! Look at the rabbit!' said Oscar, coming back into the kitchen. 'Look, everyone!' The others followed him and joined Lucy in the kitchen. They all stood together and looked over to the rabbit's cage. He was hopping about slowly, eyes wide open, nose twitching.

'The magic dust worked! Thank you, magic snow globe!' said Lucy under her breath.

'That's so good to see!' said Mum. 'He's obviously feeling a bit better. We must phone the sanctuary and ask when we can bring him over today. I'll do it now.'

'But the sanctuary is miles away. He will never get back to his own warren if we send him there,' said Lucy quickly.

'Lucy, dear,' said Gran. 'Remember—you can't just put a wild rabbit down a strange burrow and expect the other rabbits to welcome it. It takes weeks if you want to introduce a rabbit to a new warren. You have to keep it in a run in the middle of a safe field and let the wild rabbits come up and sniff it every night.'

'But what if it isn't a new warren, Gran? What if you KNOW where he comes from?'

'And do you?' said Gran.

'Not yet, but I think I can find out,' said Lucy. 'I really do, Gran.'

'Oh, Lucy,' said Gran. 'You're such a kind girl. That rabbit is lucky to have you. Look—why don't we keep him here another night? Maybe tomorrow we can find a field nearby—I could ask my friend who has helped me reintroduce rabbits before. But we do have to be careful, and we can't do anything like that if his leg is still poorly.'

'Thanks, Gran! Just let me have another night and I will try to find out where he is from.'

'How are you going to find that out, Lucy?' laughed Gran.

'I've got an idea!' said Lucy, her eyes sparkling with excitement.

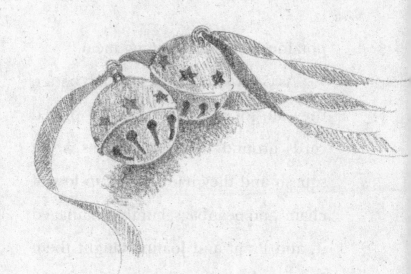

Chapter Seven

Joanna and Prajit came back from shopping with lots of goodies. Delicious smells of baking drifted in from the kitchen, and when the timer went, Dad took the cakes out and put them on the cooling rack, and popped some jacket potatoes in for the evening meal.

As Gran was feeling so much better, they all got into partners and played cards around the table. It was a big squash and they had to pull up lots of chairs and beanbags, but they managed it, and Prajit and Joanna taught them a card game Lucy's family didn't know.

'I'll be Sita's partner, shall I?' said Gran, smiling at Sita so kindly that Sita smiled back. Lucy felt a bit cross. She wanted to be Gran's partner.

'I want Lucky Lucy!' said Prajit, sitting next to her, which made her smile.

'Well, I'll have Omazing Oscar!'

said Joanna, and everyone laughed, though Oscar went a bit red.

'That just leaves me and you together,' said Mum to Dad, who pulled a silly face. Sita giggled.

'Don't worry—you're my favourite!' said Mum, giving him a kiss, and Dad pretended to go weak at the knees.

Prajit was so good at the card game that he and Lucy won, though Oscar and Joanna kept saying they were cheating. Merry came in halfway through the game. Her fur was very cold and she wound in and out of everyone's legs, purring and asking to be stroked. Joanna and Prajit and Sita all made a big fuss of her.

'She's lovely! I wish I had a cat. You're so lucky, Lucy,' Sita said shyly.

Lucy felt very proud that Merry climbed up on her lap and fell asleep.

Before they knew it, it was dinner time. They cleared the cards away and all sat around the table eating lovely hot jacket potatoes. There were lots of different fillings to choose from. Lucy had beans and cheese in hers; Sita had pineapple and cheese. Mum put out the special Christmas candles with the angels' chimes. The angels spun round in the hot air rising from the candles, and hit against the bells, making a lovely tinkling sound. It all sounded so Christmassy.

'Let's ice the cakes now,' said Mum.

'Good idea!' said Dad. 'I'll make some icing and bring in the glittery balls and toppings and we can each do our own design.'

It was a lot of fun. Dad found some icing pens and wrote 'Dad' on his, but then Prajit wrote 'No. 1 Dad' on his in even bigger letters. Mum made a snowman's smiley face, and Joanna made a Christmas tree. Oscar used up

223

loads of silver balls to make an 'O' on

his. Lucy decided to ice a picture of a

little rabbit, and when she looked over,

she was surprised to see Sita had done

the same. Sita smiled shyly at her. It was

a lovely smile and Lucy smiled back.

They had their tea and cakes by the fire in the sitting room, Merry on Gran's lap, the coloured lights on the Christmas tree twinkling. First Sita yawned, then Prajit, then Joanna.

'Oh dear—excuse us!' laughed Joanna. 'It's been such a lovely day, but I suddenly feel so tired. I think we'd better go to bed!'

'I'll just come up to make sure you have everything you need,' said Mum.

'I'll set up camp in the kitchen for the girls,' said Dad.

Lucy looked over to where she had put the snow globe on the mantelpiece.

A few snowflakes were drifting down even though nobody had shaken it. Another secret message! Lucy felt so excited she could hardly bear the wait for everyone to go to sleep so she could carry out her plan.

'Come on, Lucy, let's get Sita's bed ready,' said Dad. 'The poor girl looks half asleep already.'

So they set up two camp beds in the kitchen, Merry getting in the way again.

'I'll pop her outside if she is bothering you, shall I?' said Dad.

'No—I don't mind her,' said Sita. 'She's so sweet.' Lucy was glad. She brought the snow globe in from the sitting room and put it beside her bed.

As soon as Sita was asleep, Lucy crept over to the rabbit. There was no way to check his leg but his coat seemed shinier and his breathing had calmed down too. The kitchen was dark except for the light from the snow globe, but as Lucy pulled the pouch out of her pocket, it glowed a soft red colour in the night. When Lucy opened the pouch, the dust inside twinkled and shone like lots of beautiful tiny jewels. It was magical.

'The note said that ALL my wishes would come true, so this dust that the magic snow globe has sent me must be able to help me return you to your warren,' she said.

Lucy sprinkled the dust over the cage. It fell in a sparkling rainbow down through the bars of the cage and onto the rabbit's fur. 'I wish I knew which warren you came from,' Lucy whispered. She gasped as the rabbit opened his eyes and looked into Lucy's. His fur glittered with the magic dust, while his eyes seemed to get wider and shinier. Lucy gazed straight at him and something truly magical began to happen.

Chapter Eight

As Lucy looked into the little rabbit's eyes, the kitchen, the camp beds, and even the rabbit seemed to disappear, and all she could see was a winter field in the moonlight with lots of rabbits running around playing, nibbling the grass, and hopping around a big oak tree. There were no clouds in the sky, but lots of stars. It was beautiful. Lucy recognized the tree—she played there with Rosie sometimes. Lucy

could feel how happy and free the rabbits were together. Lucy was seeing the world through the eyes of the tiny rabbit!

Suddenly, a shadow fell across the field. It was the shadow of a big bird, hovering high up in the night sky above them, and it scared all the little rabbits. They scattered into their burrows, their tails white in the dark. Lucy's little rabbit got separated from the others and, instead of running down a burrow, he decided to run across the field to get away from the bird. He ran and ran, and Lucy could feel how frightened he was. She saw how he caught his foot on some wire as he pushed himself under a fence, and came to a busy road. In the night, the cars and the lorries were huge and noisy and their headlights dazzled the little rabbit. He was so scared of the bird, he ran across the road anyway. The cars screeched their brakes and Lucy saw the little rabbit run into an empty playing field and under a hedge, where he lay panting and all alone, as the big bird turned in the sky and flew away.

Then the pictures disappeared and Lucy was back in the kitchen, looking into the bright and shining eyes of the little rabbit. She could feel how much he longed to be back with his rabbit family in the warren.

'You poor thing,' whispered Lucy. 'You must have been so scared. And now you are far away from your friends and family. Don't worry. Thanks to the magic dust my snow globe sent me, I know exactly where your warren is. The big oak tree isn't far from here, and I'll get you home for Christmas, I promise.'

The little rabbit wiggled his nose, and Lucy knew he had heard and understood her. He lay down and closed his eyes.

Lucy sat on her bed. What could she do now? She knew EXACTLY where the little rabbit came from, but how was she going to keep her promise and get him home? Lucy crawled back into bed, determined to think of a way. It had been such a magical day. She rubbed her eyes with her hands, getting some of the glitter on her face. She looked over at Sita, sleeping peacefully. 'You've hardly said a word all day,' whispered Lucy. 'If only I knew what you were thinking.' Just then, something very strange happened. Lots of glittering rainbow colours swirled around in the air, just like the ones she had seen around the little rabbit, and instead of Sita quiet and asleep in her camp bed, Lucy could suddenly picture her laughing and playing with friends on a beach in the sun. It looked like lots of fun. There was a barbecue and Sita and her friends were running around throwing a ball. Then Lucy could see Prajit, Joanna, and Sita at a table in a house, and Sita was crying, even though her mum and dad were putting their arms around her and pointing to a calendar. Then she saw Sita and Prajit and Joanna walking up some steps to board a big plane, and lastly, Sita sitting by a window on the plane, looking out at the clouds and crying. Lucy could feel how sad and lonely she felt. Then the pictures faded.

Lucy looked down at her hands.

There was still some magic dust on them.

'Poor Sita. She feels the same way the rabbit does!' said Lucy to herself. 'Sita is sad and quiet because she misses her friends back home. I can't bring her back to Australia, but perhaps I can be her friend whilst she is here.' She looked over at Rocky in the corner. She couldn't see his kind eyes but he seemed to give a little rock as if to say, 'That's right, Lucy!'

It made Lucy feel good inside to think about helping the rabbit and Sita.

'My first two wishes came true, but I can't see how Christmas could possibly be like it used to be.' There was a tiny bit of dust in the bottom of the pouch and she turned it upside down so a few sparkling specks fell on Sita as she slept.

'I hope the magic dust gives you nice dreams,' said Lucy, and lay down in bed. 'Tomorrow will be great!' she whispered to Scruffy and Merry, and she quickly fell fast asleep cuddling them.

23rd December

'Rise and shine, sleepyheads!' came Dad's voice. 'You've slept half the morning!'

Lucy sat up with a start. The kitchen

was full of light and Dad was peeling potatoes at the sink.

'Good morning, Lucy and Sita!' said Mum, smiling down at them. 'You both slept so soundly nobody wanted to wake you, so we had breakfast in the sitting room. Oscar's off out with his friends again, and Sita's mum and dad are at the shops.'

Lucy got out of bed and rushed over to the rabbit. He was sitting up and immediately came over to the bars to sniff Lucy's hand.

'Look, Mum! Look, Sita! His leg is completely better!' said Lucy happily. 'You can't even see where it was cut now!'

Lucy gave Sita an especially big smile, as she remembered what the magic dust had shown her, and Sita smiled back and came over to join Lucy at the cage.

'Hello, bub!' said Sita softly. The little rabbit hopped over to her.

'What does that mean?' said Lucy.

'Oh, it's what we call a baby in Australia,' said Sita.

'That's what we'll call him then!' said Lucy, and they laughed. Lucy felt really good inside to see Sita looking happier.

They had boiled eggs and toast cut up into soldiers for breakfast, and

Sita taught Lucy to say more Australian words in an Australian accent, which was lots of fun.

'G'day, Gran!' said Lucy when Gran came into the room, and she and Sita got the giggles.

'Well hello, Lucy and Sita!' said Gran. 'I didn't realize you'd been to Australia overnight, Lucy!'

Lucy thought about how, in a way, she had, but she didn't say anything.

'My, that rabbit looks amazing!' said Gran. 'I can't believe it! I've never seen a leg heal like that. Perhaps it wasn't as bad as we thought. I didn't get a chance to look closely at it yesterday. You've done a wonderful job, Lucy. Sita dear, I wonder if you could come upstairs and help me with something. Maybe Lucy could help put away the beds and then join us after a bit?'

Sita went off with Gran. Lucy slipped the magic snow globe and the pouch into her dressing-gown pocket and cleared the table. Then Mum helped her fold up the beds and put them into the garage.   As soon as everything was tidied away, Lucy rushed upstairs to join Gran and Sita, pushing open the door without knocking.

'Honestly, Lucy!' said Gran, putting something behind her back. 'You really should knock before you come into a room!'

Sita turned her back and was busy putting something into a bag.

'Sorry, Gran,' said Lucy.

'That's all right, but Sita and I have something private we are doing, just the two of us, you see,' said Gran.

Lucy felt a bit hurt.

'Come back later, Lucy,' said Gran. 'Actually, we'll come and get you. Close the door behind you, there's a good girl.'

Everything was going wrong. Why was Gran being so strange?

Lucy had one hand in her pocket as she sadly went downstairs again. She took the pouch out. There was no dust left inside and it just looked like a very pretty purse. There were no wishes left.

'Maybe I can wish on the snow globe again?' she said to herself—but the snow globe looked just as it always was, and stayed cool in her hands.

So is that the end of the magic? she wondered. But as she thought that, she heard a tinkling sound, like distant bells, and little bubbles of happiness started rising inside her, driving the sadness away. She didn't know why, but she felt sure that something wonderful was just around the corner.

Chapter Nine

'I can't get over how cold it is!' said Joanna, as Lucy came into the kitchen. 'The man in the corner shop said it might even snow. How perfect! Sita has never seen snow.'

'I'd better save a carrot and we can

make a snowman in the garden if it does,' said Dad.

'A snowman! I'd really like to make one!' said Sita, coming into the kitchen with Gran.

'It's great to see you've cheered up,' said Prajit, giving her a hug. 'I was getting a bit worried about you, but ever since you woke up this morning you seem back to your old self!'

Sita smiled at Lucy, and the little bit of jealousy Lucy felt about Gran spending time with Sita disappeared. Everything was going to be fine, she could feel it.

'Who is coming to see Oscar and his

friends play football?' said Mum. 'They have a Christmas five-a-side today up at the park. We can go before lunch.'

'I'm coming!' said Gran. 'I feel so well and I'd really like a little walk and a chat with Lucy on the way,' and she took Lucy's hand. Lucy beamed.

Upstairs Lucy quickly got dressed. She took the snow globe out of her pocket and gave it a shake. The snowflakes just fell as normal, but Lucy remembered the rainbow stars she had seen, and what she had seen in the little rabbit's eyes.

'I've got to trust in the globe—it promised me my wishes would come true, it sent me the magic dust, and I know it showed me where Bub comes from,' Lucy decided. 'I'm going to ask Gran if I can take Bub back to the field with the oak tree tonight. I hope she agrees,' she said to herself.

'Come on, Lucy!' called Dad up the stairs. 'I don't want to miss Oscar score the winning goal!'

They all set out for the short walk to the park. The sky was a cold slate grey and Lucy was glad she had her hat, coat, scarf, and gloves on.

'I can't believe how well the rabbit

looks!' said Gran, as they walked along together. 'I was wondering if you could show me where you found him.'

'Gran! If I could tell you where his warren is, would it be too late to take him back? I think I know where it is, Gran!' said Lucy, swinging her gran's arm excitedly. 'Can I show you?'

'Well, Oscar and his friends don't seem to have started properly yet, so let's have a look,' said Gran.

Lucy took Gran and Sita to the hedge where she had found the rabbit, and then they crossed the road to another field with a big oak tree. Lucy tried to remember what the rabbit had showed her, and she looked for the bit of the fence he had squeezed under and caught his foot on.

'Look, Gran! Here is a little bit of fur. This is where Bub caught his foot— I am sure of it! I think he was running from a bird of prey. And look, Gran— look what is in the field!'

Gran looked over. 'Well,' she said, 'the fur on the fence is rabbit fur. It definitely looks like there is a warren there—look at all the entrances to the burrows! It would make sense that this is where he came from . . . If only we could be sure . . .'

'Gran, please can we bring Bub here

tonight when it is dusk and the rabbits come out? Please. I'm sure we will know for sure then,' said Lucy.

'Oh! Please can I come too?' said Sita excitedly. 'I'd really like to see little Bub go home!'

'Well, perhaps if your dad drives us here, Lucy, and your mum and dad agree you can come, Sita. But if I don't think we are doing the right thing, and it looks like the other rabbits are going to fight Bub, then we will bring him back home with us. All right, girls?' said Gran.

'All right,' said Lucy. She just had to hope that the magic snow globe would fix things.

They watched the football match. Will and Oscar scored a goal each and Fergus did a brilliant save so that in the end their team won and Oscar was very happy. Then they all came home for hot soup and rolls and lots of cheese, and in the afternoon they played Scrabble. Oscar made the words 'ball' and 'goal', and everyone laughed. Gran found the letters for 'bunny' and Lucy spelt 'home' and they smiled at each other.

'Could you drive Lucy and Sita and me up to the field across the road from the park tonight?' said Gran to Lucy's dad. 'We are going to have a little adventure and see if we can return the rabbit home. It looks like the nearest warren.'

'Oh, please can I go?' said Sita to her mum and dad. 'He's such a sweet rabbit. I'd like to see him back with his friends.'

Lucy remembered the magic pictures of Sita she had seen. Sita needed friends as much as the rabbit.

'What do you think?' said Gran. 'Can Sita come?'

'Please—I'd love Sita to come too!' said Lucy, and as she said it, she found that she meant it.

'Of course!' said Joanna and Prajit, smiling.

'Thank you!' said Sita, and the next word she made in Scrabble was 'friend'.

'Look!' she said to Lucy, and Lucy felt very happy. Sita was going to live in her village, and Lucy suddenly knew she would be a good friend. She couldn't wait for her to meet Rosie

Just as it was dusk, Dad drove them to the field with the rabbit in the cage.

Lucy could feel how hopeful and excited he was getting as they got nearer. His little nose was twitching, and his eyes were shining happily. She had the snow globe in her pocket and she held it tightly.

'Please make it all right for little Bub,' she wished.

They all got out of the car, and Lucy and Sita helped Dad and Gran carry the cage over the stile into the field. The evening mist was hanging in the air, and it all felt very still and magical as they walked across the field under the grey snow clouds. They could see lots of little white tails disappear into burrows as they walked nearer to the warren. The little rabbit was very alert, sitting up in the cage.

'What do we do now?' asked Dad.

'Well, we put the cage down and see what happens,' said Gran. 'We'll walk back to the car so the rabbits can't see us and we'll watch from there. The cage door is locked so he will be safe if they don't accept him.'

They put the cage down, and Lucy looked into the little rabbit's eyes. He was so sweet, and she knew she would miss him, but she could feel how excited and happy he was to be back in his field.

'Bye, Bub!' said Sita. 'Hope you find your friends!'

'Bye-bye, little rabbit,' whispered Lucy. 'Have a happy Christmas!'

Then they walked back to the car and turned back to look.

'My goodness!' said Gran. 'I've never seen anything like it!'

Chapter Ten

All around the cage were lots and lots of rabbits. The little rabbit was looking out at them and scrabbling at the cage as if he wanted to get out.

'Oh dear. I hope he won't hurt himself,' said Gran, 'I think we should go back.'

There was a little flash of sparkling rainbow colour over where the cage was.

'What was that?' said Dad, puzzled.

It's the last of the magic dust! Lucy thought happily. It's the final part of the wish coming true.

Then they saw the cage door fly open and the little rabbit run out!

'Oh no!' said Gran worriedly. 'I can't have locked it properly.' But soon she was smiling. The rabbits were nuzzling each other and hopping around, and the little rabbit was in the middle of the group, totally at home. He sat for a minute on his back legs and looked

in their direction as if to say thank you. Lucy made eye contact with him.

'Good luck, Bub!' she whispered, and she knew deep down that he had understood.

Then, with a flash of white tail, Bub and all the others disappeared back down into the burrows.

'Well, that was a big success!' said Dad. 'I thought it was much harder than that normally.'

'It is,' said Gran, looking puzzled. 'But I suppose it IS Christmas and everyone knows magical things happen at this time of year!' She reached over and gave Lucy and Sita a big hug. 'That little rabbit looked so well—you really have a special gift with animals, Lucy.'

Sita and Lucy sat in the back of the car with the empty rabbit cage wedged between them as they drove home.

'Bub was so lovely,' said Sita, 'but I'm glad he is back with his friends.'

'When my friend Rosie comes back from her Grandad's, you can meet her,' said Lucy. 'We'll all be in the same class at school. I know you miss your friends back in Australia, Sita, but can we be your friends whilst you are here?'

'I'd like that, Lucy!' said Sita. 'I think England will be fun.'

That night, Lucy and Sita played

with Lucy's Christmas puppet theatre before they went to bed. Sita loved the little baby reindeer figure. Lucy put the snow globe back next to her bed. It was as pretty as ever, but somehow it didn't look magical any more, and when Lucy touched it, there was no special tingly feeling.

Perhaps all the magic's used up now - and anyhow there's no more magic dust, thought Lucy. *But I'm glad not all my wishes came true. I wanted Christmas to be like it always is, but that didn't happen—and it's better! I love being friends with Sita—and I know Rosie will too. I'm so happy that wish WASN'T granted!*

Chapter Eleven

24th December

The next day was Christmas Eve, and full of fun. Mum took Lucy to the Christmas market and they bought a tiny snow globe with a rabbit in for Sita's Christmas present.

In the afternoon they all went off

into secret places around the house and wrapped presents, so that the pile of packages by the Christmas tree got higher and higher. Merry got far too excited and tried to

climb it, so they had to put her in the kitchen with an early present—a special cat activity centre with tunnels and posts and toy mice hanging down on strings. Merry absolutely loved batting them with her paws.

At night they went off to church to hear Christmas carols by candlelight, and as they walked home, they felt something cold and light and feathery on their faces.

'Is it snow?' asked Sita.

'Yes!' said Lucy.

'I had such a lovely dream about it snowing at Christmas!' Sita said happily.

25th December

Christmas Day came, and everywhere was dusted with snow.

'How pretty!' said Sita, as she

woke up. 'I'm so glad to be here for Christmas!'

'I'm glad you're here too!' said Lucy.

They had a special breakfast of delicious pastries and croissants and some yummy Italian panettone cake. Then they all gathered around the Christmas tree to open their presents. Joanna and Prajit had brought some really fun things—Lucy and Oscar each had a boomerang, Mum had a brooch in the shape of a kangaroo, Gran had one in the shape of a koala, and Dad had a didgeridoo, a musical instrument like a decorated wooden drainpipe.

'I kept it hidden in the car boot as I thought you'd guess,' laughed Prajit. 'I'll teach you to play it!'

'Oh no! Prajit is the world's worst player!' groaned Joanna.

'Not now Dad has one!' said Oscar.

'Cheeky boy!' said Dad, 'I've had a go at one before—listen!' He blew into it and managed to make a very loud deep humming note from the instrument, which made little Merry jump and run behind a chair. She peeped out crossly until Lucy picked her up and gave her a cuddle.

'Thank you,' said Sita as she unwrapped her snow globe. 'It's lovely!'

'Lucy—this is from me,' Gran said, handing her a soft parcel. 'But before I give it to you, I want to make a special announcement!'

Everyone stopped talking and opening their presents to listen.

'As you know, I'm much better now that my shoulder has been fixed, so I have decided that I am going to open my Wildlife Rescue Centre again in the New Year. I don't think I will be able to do it on my own without an assistant, though, and after talking to your mum and dad, I would like it to be you, Lucy. You have a very special gift with animals, and I would like you to work with me during the holidays and when you have time at the weekends. This will explain your present.'

Lucy unwrapped it. Merry immediately jumped all over the paper as Lucy lifted out a very special red sweatshirt.

'Sita was very kind and helped me finish it off, as I couldn't sew as much as I wanted when I was in hospital. I'm sorry if we rushed you out of your room, but that's what we were hiding from you the other day,' said Gran. 'This is your uniform. There is the special Wildlife Rescue Centre logo on the front, and on the top of the sleeve, look what there is . . .'

Lucy looked, and saw it was a badge with a lovely embroidered rabbit.

'It's lovely!' she said.

'Every time you look after an animal I will embroider a new badge for you to put on your uniform, so everyone can see what a kind and clever animal lover you are!' said Gran, giving her a kiss.

Lucy beamed with pride. 'Thank you so much, Gran! I'd LOVE to be your assistant at the Centre! I can't think of anything better!

That night, Lucy lay in her camp bed in the kitchen, cuddling Scruffy. Merry was asleep at her feet, and Sita was asleep in her bed, but Lucy lay awake, shaking the snow globe and thinking about what a lovely day they had had. She thought about Christmas dinner, with everyone crowded round trying to pull crackers and laughing, and Dad setting fire to the Christmas pudding, and how funny everyone looked in their hats. She thought about the snow rabbit that was in the garden. She and Sita had managed to make it after Christmas dinner, and the others had built a funny snowman next to it. Sita was definitely going to be a very special friend.

'I just wish I knew how our rabbit is,' she said to Scruffy and Rocky, and as she said it, the snow globe glowed one last time, and suddenly, Lucy saw her rabbit in the snow globe, looking up at her.

He looked so sweet and happy, as if he was smiling.

'Thank you,' she felt him say to her.

His little ears gave a twitch and he turned and disappeared. The globe showed her one last picture—a little pile of sleeping rabbits curled up cosy and warm together in a burrow. One raised his head and looked at her and she knew it was hers, and that he was safe and home.

'Thank you, magic snow globe, and goodnight, little Bub,' Lucy whispered, and with a sound of sleigh bells the picture inside the globe went back to being a pretty little house in a wood, with the snow falling. 'Happy Christmas!'

LUCY'S WINTER RESCUE

Written by
Anne Booth

Illustrated by
Sophy Williams

OXFORD
UNIVERSITY PRESS

To Oliver, Thea, Adam, and Esme
And to Theo and Saffy Haynes

Chapter One

It was the week before Christmas, and Lucy and her friend Sita had gone to play at their friend Rosie's house for the afternoon.

It was always fun at Rosie's. She lived in a house by the river with her mum, and her stepdad, Peter. Peter and her mum had a little baby, so Rosie had a little sister, Leah. Everybody loved Leah. She was only two and a half and loved dressing up and playing with Rosie and her friends. Today Leah wanted to be Father Christmas's baby reindeer and

live under the table, so the girls took it in turns to pretend to feed her and give her lots of special hugs. She was so sweet.

'Me baby rabbit now!' said Leah, coming out from under the table, jumping around the room.

'Leah would love my gran's Wildlife Rescue Centre!' laughed Lucy. 'We have a wild rabbit with a sore ear there now.'

'She'd love your uniform and the badges your gran makes for it too!' laughed Rosie. 'What animal badges have you got now?'

'Well, I've got badges for helping a magpie with a broken wing, and a newt, and we're looking after lots of tiny hedgehogs, so Gran is making me a hedgehog badge. I've got my rabbit badge already because of the little baby rabbit I rescued last Christmas.'

'That was when I had just arrived from Australia,' said Sita. 'I remember that little rabbit!'

'Me RABBIT!' shouted Leah.

'Why don't you be a sleeping bunny?' said Rosie, and she played a song on the piano about little bunnies being asleep.

'Everybody sleeping bunnies!' said Leah, and she made Lucy and Sita lie down beside her and pretend to be asleep. Leah looked very sweet and Lucy made Sita laugh by pretending to snore.

Then, when Rosie sang the waking up words 'Hop little bunny, hop, hop, hop!', Lucy and Sita had to jump up and down with Leah, who thought it was the best fun ever and kept hopping and hopping and laughing and laughing so that they all laughed too.

'Again! Again!' said Leah, but just at that moment, Rosie's mum came in.

'Thanks so much for playing with Leah, girls, but I think she might need a little nap now.'

'NO!' shouted Leah. 'Me bunny. Me HOP. Me not go bed.' Her face went very red and she started to cry.

'Girls—I don't think she will settle if

she thinks you are in the house. Do you think you could go and find some holly and ivy for me? I saw quite a lot growing next to the river the other day. I thought we might use it to help decorate the church for Christmas, and you can bring back some for your homes if you like. I'll give you some scissors and some thick gloves and this bag to put them in. Now girls, be careful not to get too near the river—it's got a lot higher lately. I think it's all the rain we've been having. I know you'll be sensible.'

The girls put on their warm coats and hats and scarves and went down Rosie's garden to her back gate and out on to

the wide path by the river. They could still hear little Leah's wailing: 'No! No sleep! Want GIRLS! Want DOGGY!'

'What does she mean?' said Sita. 'You don't have a dog.'

'She keeps saying there's a dog in the garden,' said Rosie. 'But we've never seen one.'

'Poor Leah—she sounds so upset,' said Lucy.

'She'll be all right after her nap,' said Rosie, closing the gate behind her. 'She just got a bit too excited doing that song.'

'You're such a good singer,' said Sita.

'Um,' said Rosie, and made a face.

'What's the matter?' said Lucy.

'It's just that Mum and I are in the church choir, and we're going to sing carols at Forest Lodge—the old people's home my grandad's in. We're going to sing to them on Christmas Eve—and they want me to sing a solo.'

'That's great!' said Sita.

'You're so good at music! You'll be brilliant!' said Lucy.

Rosie bit her lip. 'I don't know—I'm just really worried. What if it all goes wrong and I let everyone down? Grandad has been telling everyone in the home about my singing. Mum and Peter say I will be fine, and even Dad is coming to see me. But what if I forget the words or sing out of tune? I'm so scared I keep having bad dreams and waking up and worrying about it.'

Just then Lucy heard a strange little cry coming from the riverbank—a faint, very high-pitched call, a bit like a cross between a whistle and a whimper.

'Did you hear that?' she said. A red-breasted robin hopped on to a bush nearby and started singing.

'That's a robin,' said Sita. 'That's so Christmassy!'

'No, I meant the first noise. Listen.' The girls stopped. The faint high noise came again, along with some tiny splashes.

'It's coming from those reeds on the riverbank near us,' said Lucy.

'Is it a water vole?' said Rosie. 'I remember you told us Ratty in *The Wind in the Willows* was one.'

'I don't think it's a water vole,' said Lucy, turning in the direction of the cries and carefully making her way down the riverbank. 'I'd love to see one but Gran and I have looked and there are no burrows or droppings or tracks along this bit of the river. There are no feeding stations either, where they leave piles of stems of grass. But I think I may have an idea what it is. I think this animal is in *The Wind in the Willows* too. I just hope it isn't in trouble.'

'Be very careful,' said Rosie. 'Mum told us to stay away from the river.'

Lucy reached the riverbank, and peered into the reeds right at the edge. At first she could only see some rubbish—a crisp packet and a beer can—but then . . .

'Oh no!' said Lucy. 'This is awful. Can you pass me the gloves and the scissors, Rosie?'

Rosie and Sita carefully made their way down the bank to where Lucy was, and looked over her shoulder into the reeds. There, struggling to keep its head above the water, and trapped in the reeds, with some plastic rubbish around its neck, was a small furry animal.

'I was right—it's a baby otter!' said Lucy. 'I've never seen one so small. Gran told me they stay in their holt—that's their home—for about three months, so this one shouldn't be out alone at all. We've got to get it out of those reeds and keep it warm—look how it's shivering.'

'What should we do?' said Sita.

'I'm going to put on the thick gloves,' Lucy replied. 'It looks too tiny and weak to bite me but I'm not taking any chances: I know otter teeth are really sharp. Gran told me about a friend of hers who had to go to hospital when a grown-up otter bit her. Then I'm going to lift it out and hold it and you can cut the plastic off from around its neck.'

Lucy put on the gloves and lifted

the baby otter out. Lucy had learned from
her gran how to hold animals gently but
firmly so they couldn't bite. Sita carefully
cut the plastic off its neck. It was too weak

to struggle much and its poor little neck looked sore. Its fur was dark and sodden, and it was shivering.

'Here,' said Rosie, taking off her hat and scarf. 'Let's wrap it up and bring it home quickly. You can ring your gran from my house, Lucy.'

'It's very ill,' said Lucy, as they rushed back up the path. 'It might not even know how to swim yet—they don't learn until they are about ten weeks old and they are blind until they are four or five weeks old. Gran was teaching me about them last night. I didn't think I'd see one so soon. I wonder how old this one is.'

Back at Rosie's house, Lucy called

Gran and told her what they had found. Gran headed over straight away. Rosie found a cardboard box and a towel. They unwrapped the baby otter from Rosie's hat and scarf and tried to blot the excess water from its dark fur. It kept its eyes closed and didn't struggle.

'I'm so sorry girls, but it's very ill,' said Gran. 'It is so small—about nine weeks old—that I think the river water must have risen and washed this little cub out of its holt and downstream, and into the reeds and the rubbish. It shouldn't be outside yet. And it is so cold and that awful plastic has rubbed against its poor little neck and made it sore. I'll bring it back to the Centre now and I'll phone the vet. I think it will need an antibiotic injection to help it fight any infection it may have.'

Rosie and Sita looked upset. 'We're going to save it!' said Lucy confidently. 'I know we can. I'll go back with Gran now but I'll tell you all about it tomorrow—I promise.'

Lucy picked up the box and whispered, so that only the otter could hear. 'Don't worry—I have a magic snow globe and as soon as I get home I am going to wish on it for you. You'll be better for Christmas—I know you will!'

Chapter Two

Gran and Lucy went back to Gran's house, and went through to the Wildlife Rescue Centre at the back. Even though it was a working sanctuary it still looked Christmassy—Lucy had made and hung up some red and silver and green and gold paper chains along the walls, and Gran had put up a Christmas tree in the corner with little animal treats wrapped up in Christmas paper hanging from the branches.

The rabbit with a sore ear hopped to the side of its cage and wiggled its nose as they came in; a sleeping owl that had hurt its leg opened its eyes and closed them again; and the five little hedgehogs snuffled around in their special cages.

'Take that warm towel from the radiator, Lucy,' said Gran, 'and put it on the bottom of this heated cage. Check the cage temperature is about 30°C. We don't want to overheat him but he needs to get warm. He won't feed if he is cold.'

Then Gran carefully lifted the sick little otter and placed him into the cage.

'Will he be OK, Gran?' Lucy said. She didn't feel so confident anymore. He looked so poorly and his breathing wasn't very good. Lucy felt her eyes fill with tears. It was so sad to see him looking so ill.

'I don't know, Lucy, love, but I hope so,' said Gran. 'I'll ring the vet. He's in the warm and dry now. There is not much we can do now for him until he warms up a bit.'

I know something I can do, thought Lucy suddenly. 'I'll be back in five minutes, Gran,' she said, and ran out of the house.

303

Lucy ran as fast as she could back to her house and up the stairs to her bedroom. There, beside her bed, was her snow globe. It was a beautiful glass globe with a forest and a little house inside,

and when she shook it snow fell—but Lucy knew that sometimes it had a way of making special things happen, and she hoped so much that it could help her now.

'I know there's something magic about you at Christmas,' said Lucy, sitting on the bed and picking it up. 'And it's Christmas time now and I really need you to do magic. PLEASE magic snow globe—help that poor little otter get better.' She closed her eyes as she made her wish and shook the globe. She had shaken it many times during the year and nothing magic had happened—but now as she shook it she felt her hands tingling as it grew warm. It was working! She opened her eyes and she saw the snow falling inside the globe start to glow and whirl and sparkle and change from white to silver, green, and red and all the different colours of the rainbow.

Suddenly the glittering snow cleared completely and even the house and the wood disappeared. Instead, for a moment she was sure she saw in the globe a little red car driving down a road and stopping outside her gran's door. She blinked, and the car and Gran's house had gone. All she could see was white snow falling on a little house in a wood again. It was almost as if she had imagined it. But her hands still tingled and inside she suddenly felt extremely happy, as if someone had told her a most wonderful secret . . . she wasn't sure what it was but she knew it was good.

She quickly pulled on her Wildlife Rescue Centre sweatshirt, put the globe in her coat pocket, and rushed back to Gran's. As she got there Gran was just waving off a little red car. It was the same car Lucy had seen in her snow globe!

'You'll never guess what happened, Lucy!' said Gran, smiling. 'Just after you left, before I even got through to the surgery, the vet called by with a Christmas card. She took a look at the otter and she gave him an injection of antibiotics. She said that you found him just in time, as he could have given up struggling and drowned, and that the antibiotics will help him. I can't help feeling he looks better already!'

The snow globe granted my wish, thought Lucy excitedly as she watched the baby otter. He seemed to like it in the warm, stretching his little legs out. He gave a

little wriggle. Lucy watched and saw his fur begin to dry out, changing colour from dark to light brown, spiking a little like a hedgehog.

'He's so sweet!' said Lucy, peering in.

'He is—but if we can get him to pull through he needs rehoming somewhere else quickly,' said Gran. 'If we raise him on his own he will be too used to humans and follow us about.'

'But wouldn't it be lovely if we could have a pet otter?' said Lucy. 'Imagine him following me to school—all the children would want one!'

'Not when he got older, Lucy,' said Gran. 'Their teeth are very sharp and their jaws are very powerful. They can bite and badly hurt people even without meaning to. They are shy, mysterious, beautiful animals. They need other otters and wild spaces and water.'

Lucy looked in at the little otter. 'Do you think we can get him back home before Christmas?'

'I'm not sure we'll be able to find his home, Lucy. We don't know where he has come from. The flooded river may have swept him down into the village from the wilder countryside. Even if we found his holt nearer the village then we couldn't be sure it was his, and we can't approach it and disturb any other otters in it. We need to find an otter sanctuary as soon as possible. I'll give my old friend, Tom, a call this afternoon—we used to work together in his otter sanctuary. I do hope he'll be able to help.'

'While the little otter is at the Centre could I help look after him as well as the tiny hedgehogs?'

'Of course! And then I will give you an otter badge to go with the hedgehog badge and the others. You're so good at looking after animals, Lucy. Look at how much weight the little hedgehogs have put on since you started helping! We'll be able to release them into safe gardens in the spring and they will go back to eating the slugs and helping the lucky gardeners. Then next winter they will be fat enough to hibernate. They will sleep through until the following spring thanks to all your hard work.'

Lucy beamed. She loved learning about wildlife from Gran. Normally she wore her special uniform when she came to clean out the cages or feed the animals. In the winter they had lots of baby or underweight hedgehogs who were too small to hibernate. They needed feeding and keeping warm, and each time they put a hedgehog on the scales it was Lucy's job to carefully write down in a book how much it weighed. It was lovely to feel and see them getting heavier.

The otter wriggled and made a tiny weak chittering noise.

'Can I feed it?' said Lucy. 'What will it eat, Gran?'

'It's still very tiny, so we will give it a syringe of glucose and water first, and then the special puppy-rearing milk will be fine. We can mix it with a little raw, flaked fish and feed it from a spoon— and we will have to do it every hour at first. It will be a lot of work.'

'I'll help!' said Lucy eagerly.

Gran held the otter as Lucy syringed a little liquid into his mouth. He seemed to like the taste and opened his dark eyes a little. Then he lapped a bit of the fish and puppy milk mixture from the spoon Lucy held out.

'That's a very good sign,' said Gran. When the little otter was tired and had finished eating, Lucy helped Gran clean his sore neck. They made sure he had gone to the toilet and then popped him back snugly in his box. Gran found a hot-water bottle with a furry cover to put in the box and the little cub snuggled up next to it, closed his eyes, and went to sleep.

Chapter Three

The rest of the afternoon went very
quickly—every hour they fed the little
otter, and there was always so much to do
looking after the birds and other animals
and keeping their cages and bowls
clean. Lucy put on some rubber gloves

and did some washing up, and washed and disinfected the surfaces. Then she checked the shelves to see what new things Gran needed to reorder.

'We need more mealworms and milk formula, more kitchen roll and disposable aprons, and more gloves and bandages, Gran,' she said, writing a list on the board.

'Well, Christmas is coming—maybe Father Christmas will bring them!' said Gran, sighing. 'It does cost so much to keep this going.' Then she smiled and gave Lucy a big hug.

'Wash your hands and then off you go home, Lucy. I'll keep an eye on everything. Thank you so much. You've been such a help today.'

Lucy walked home feeling tired but happy. Her house looked very Christmassy—outside Dad had put up coloured fairy lights which twinkled on and off, and Mum had hung a Christmas

wreath on the door. Inside it was full of tinsel decorations, Christmas cards were everywhere, and the pile of Christmas presents under the tree was getting bigger every day.

Lucy didn't have much chance to tell her family about the otter at first because her brother Oscar's team had won a football match, and he had to tell everybody every detail of every goal over dinner. Lucy kept trying to interrupt but Oscar was too interested in his story to notice—he kept waving his arms and moving the snowmen salt and pepper pots around the table to show who moved where and when.

'That's great, Oscar, well done,' said Lucy's dad eventually. 'I think maybe we should ask Lucy about her day now.'

'Rosie and Sita and I rescued a baby otter today,' said Lucy.

'Where did you find it?' said Oscar. 'They are normally very hard to find. Are you sure it wasn't a stoat or a weasel?'

Oscar's so annoying sometimes, thought Lucy. *Just because he goes to secondary school he thinks he knows everything.*

'Yes, I am sure!' replied Lucy. 'Gran thinks it must have been swept out of its holt by flood waters, and then it got tangled up in some plastic rubbish in the river behind Rosie's house. Its neck is really sore.'

'That's awful,' said Oscar. 'People shouldn't throw rubbish in the river— it's really dangerous for wildlife.' Lucy stopped feeling so cross. Oscar could be a bit bossy, and his football stories were too long, but he was kind. Lucy could see that Merry, her cat, had crept under the table and was sitting on Oscar's feet, and he was letting her.

'How were Rosie and Sita?' said Mum.

'They're fine, but Rosie's very worried about singing in the concert at the old people's home on Christmas Eve. She's doing a solo,' said Lucy.

'I'm sure she'll be wonderful,' said Dad. 'I've heard her sing and I'd pay to hear her! Tell her not to worry.'

After dinner Lucy felt so tired she went to bed early. She got her snow globe out of her coat pocket and brought it back upstairs and put it next to her bed. Merry followed her up to her room as usual. Sometimes Merry went out at night, but she always started the night on Lucy's bed, and she was always there when Lucy woke in the morning.

Lucy brushed her teeth and put on her pyjamas. Then she got into bed next to Scruffy, her pyjama-case dog, and Merry. She shook the globe again and they watched the snow fall over the little Christmas scene of a cottage in a snowy wood. She felt very sleepy.

'Thank you so much, snow globe, for sending the vet to the otter,' said Lucy. 'Gran and I will look after him and feed him and keep him warm until he is better.'

She was sure the snow globe felt warm in her hands and glowed brightly for a moment, but her eyes felt so tired they kept closing.

'Did you see that?' she said to Merry, Scruffy, and her rocking horse, Rocky, as she put the snow globe on her bedside table. Merry pushed her head against

Lucy's arm and purred, but Lucy wasn't sure if she was just trying to get her to lie down so Merry could tuck in comfortably behind her. Lucy yawned.

'Goodnight, you three. I hope the little otter and Rosie sleep well tonight,' she said. It was nice to see the snow globe back on the bedside table at Christmas, and she was certain it had sent the vet to the otter. Lucy yawned and lay down and fell fast asleep, Merry snuggled up behind her, the snow in the snow globe still falling over the trees and the little house, even though Lucy had stopped shaking it a long time before.

Chapter 4

'Hello Merry!' said Lucy, early the next morning. The little cat looked very sweet and comfortable stretched out on her back on Lucy's bed. Lucy stroked her soft furry tummy but Merry quickly curled on her side, keeping her eyes tightly shut, her paws still soft and her claws in, but her tail twitching a little.

'Sleepyhead!' laughed Lucy. 'OK, I'll let you sleep—but I'm going to get up. I want to see how the little otter is.'

She reached over to the snow globe and shook it. The snow drifted down and it looked very pretty as usual, but there was no magic glow or tingly feeling in her hands.

Lucy pulled on her cosy dressing gown and ran downstairs for breakfast. She loved the Christmas holidays.

'Can I go and help Gran with the otter cub, Mum?' she asked, as she spread butter on her toast.

'Of course!' laughed Mum. 'Be back for lunch at one, though. Sita and her mum and dad are coming round.'

After breakfast Lucy put on her Wildlife Rescue Centre uniform, grabbed her coat, and rushed over to Gran's. She went through the garden gate, straight through to the Centre, where she found Gran already cleaning out the cages.

'Hello, Lucy!' said Gran. 'You're just in time to help me feed the otter.' Gran and Lucy washed their hands and put on disposable gloves.

'He's much perkier now,' said Gran as they pulled the cardboard box out of the heated cage. The little otter put his short webbed feet over the side and looked at them with interest.

'I love his little whiskers!' said Lucy. 'And his tiny ears! He looks so solemn!'

'Let's find out how much he weighs,' said Gran, putting the little otter on the scales. The tiny creature wasn't quite sure what to do but luckily he stayed still long enough, his paws spread wide, for Gran to read his weight; then Lucy caught him just as he tried to scramble off, his long tail swishing.

Lucy was used to holding small animals, and, although the otter was very wriggly, she held him close whilst Gran got the feed ready. Then Lucy fed the little otter some mashed-up salmon and puppy milk formula from the spoon. He was very hungry and closed his eyes, concentrating on every mouthful. Gran had to hold him very firmly as his little paws kept reaching up to get the spoon and nearly knocked it out of Lucy's hands. His long tail moved from side to side in excitement.

'We'll clean his neck up again, but it is looking so much better already,' said Gran. 'I'll put him in this little playpen so he can have a run around in safety—and he can sleep in the cat basket. Can you put a soft towel in it?'

Gran refilled the hot-water bottle

and put it in the cat basket. 'I have a little soft teddy he can cuddle up with, but he really needs to be with other otters as soon as possible, poor little thing!' she said. 'But first I'll hold him over the cat litter tray. Do you remember what I told you otter poo was called, Lucy?'

'Spraint,' said Lucy.

'Yes. They use it to mark their territory too. It might be interesting to go back down along the river this afternoon and see if we can see any spraint or paw prints in the mud,' said Gran. 'I wonder how far this little fellow was washed down river? It is so good you found him, Lucy, and that you got that rubbish off his neck in time.'

'I hate rubbish,' said Lucy. 'I remember that poor hedgehog we found with his head stuck in a plastic bag—he would have died if we hadn't found him. I don't know why people don't throw their rubbish away.'

'It isn't just rubbish, either,' said Gran, putting the little otter down in the playpen next to a ball. 'Otters get very ill from a disease they catch from cats—but they don't get it from meeting cats. They get it when people flush cat litter down the toilet instead of putting it in the bin. The disease gets into the water system and rivers, and otters are very sensitive to it and can even die.'

'That's awful!' said Lucy. 'I didn't know that. I'm going to tell everyone at school that cat litter should be put in the bin, not down the loo.'

'That would be wonderful, Lucy!' said Gran. 'If people just stopped doing that and were more careful about rubbish that would help otters a lot.'

The little otter rolled on top of the ball and pushed it around a little with his paws. Gran put down a long cardboard tube and he squeezed himself in and out, chittering excitedly.

'He's so lovely,' said Lucy. 'Should we put him in a bath so he can swim about?'

Gran laughed. 'Lucy, as he hasn't yet learned to swim, he would HATE it! When I worked in the otter sanctuary with my friend Tom, I remember the amount of noise there was when we first put rescued baby otters in water. They squeaked so long and loudly! It's hard to believe but in the wild the otter mums have to be quite firm with their cubs. No, I think we'll leave that job to the otter sanctuary. I do hope Tom returns my call soon. This cub really needs to be with other otters and it would be too easy to fall in love with him here. Look.'

The excited little otter had fallen asleep on the floor of the pen. Lucy climbed over and picked him up carefully and put him in the cat basket next to his teddy and cosy hot-water bottle.

'He'll be fine for another few hours,' said Gran. 'All the birds and animals are sorted for now. I think I'll have some lunch and put my feet up for a bit. It's such a lovely winter's day maybe I'll go out for a walk later.'

'Or a paddle?' said Lucy. 'Gran, I was thinking—maybe if some of us went to the river near Rosie's we could pull out the rubbish that is in the reeds and stop another little river animal or bird getting hurt. Sita and her mum and dad are coming for lunch—maybe they could help.'

'That's a good idea, Lucy! Our Christmas present to the river!' said Gran. 'Give me a ring when you go down there and I'll get my long wader boots and join you. It shouldn't take too long if there is a team of us.'

Lucy ran home and got there just in time to change out of her uniform and into her favourite reindeer jumper, wash her hands, and join Sita and her parents at lunch. Oscar's friends, Will and Fergus, were round and Dad and Mum said they could stay for pizza too, so the kitchen was very crowded. Mum said the children could take their lunch into the sitting room and watch television.

'I wish there was some football on,' complained Oscar. 'I don't feel like watching a Christmas film or anything like that.'

There was a cartoon about a little kitten and a programme about someone building their own house, but Oscar flicked through the channels.

'Hey! Wait!' said Fergus. 'That's an otter!'

It was a programme about a family who lived near a river, and they were

watching a group of otters swim together. The family could only see their heads as they looked above the water, and the bubbles on the surface as they dived underneath the surface of the river. The programme said how mysterious and shy wild otters are and how hard they are to spot. Luckily there were underwater cameras in the river itself, and so the programme showed how the otters chased fish in the river, and how they all twisted and turned and rolled together under the water. Baby otters didn't like learning to swim, but by the time they were adults they were experts.

'It's so beautiful!' said Sita.

'They have so much fun together,' said Lucy, feeling sad to think of the little otter all on his own. She wondered if she could ask the snow globe for another wish.

'I love otters,' said Fergus. 'I used to have a great book called *Tarka the Otter*.'

'So did I!' said Oscar. 'And Gran adopted an otter for me for one year when I was five.'

'I didn't know that!' said Lucy. 'That's a lovely present! I'd like that!'

'Yes—I remember it lived at the otter sanctuary she used to work at and I used to get letters and photographs from it.'

'I didn't know otters could write!'

said Will, and Oscar threw a cushion at him, narrowly missing the Christmas tree.

'Mind my pizza!' said Will.

'We rescued an otter cub yesterday,' said Lucy. 'It was tangled up in rubbish in the river, so Gran and I are going to clear out rubbish this afternoon so that no more otters or birds get hurt. I was going to ask if people would come and help. If lots of us go it shouldn't take long at all.'

'I'll help,' said Sita.

'So will I,' said Fergus. 'Me too,' said Will, 'as long as there's time to play football afterwards.'

'Who said anything about football?' said Sita's dad, standing at the door. 'Did you hear that, Sita?'

'Can we help Lucy's gran clear out the river near Rosie's house?' said Sita. 'It will only be for an hour or so.'

'That's a good idea,' said Sita's mum. 'It's such a lovely day it will be good to get some fresh air.'

'I'll see if I have any spare wellies for anyone to borrow,' said Mum.

'And I think I have some fishing trousers I can lend too,' said Dad. 'We don't want anyone going for a bath!'

'I'll ring Rosie,' said Lucy. 'I'll tell her how the little otter is and about operation Christmas clean-up! It's going to be fun!'

Chapter Five

Rosie opened the door and led Lucy and the gang through to the kitchen. Gran was already there chatting to Rosie's mum. Leah was standing up with a Christmas apron on, helping her mum stir some cake mixture, but as soon as she saw everyone she wanted to join them. She especially liked the funny Christmas hat Lucy's dad was wearing, even though Lucy and Oscar had begged him not to wear it outside the house.

'Lucy Daddy funny hat!' she cried. And 'Me go too!', dropping her spoon in the bowl.

'But Leah—we're making chocolate cake now. You like making cakes,' said her mum. 'We'll make it into a log and decorate it.'

'Me no cake. STOPPIT!' said Leah firmly, trying to pull her apron off.

'Oh dear,' sighed Rosie's mum. 'I suppose I'll get on quicker if Leah is with you—but you will keep an eye on her, won't you, Rosie? Keep her away from the water. You can use her safety reins— she likes them at the moment if she can pretend she is a horse or a dog.'

'She can be a special reindeer if she likes,' said Lucy. 'Would you like that, Leah?' Leah nodded and carefully got off the chair. Sita helped her take off her apron and Rosie brought her yellow duck wellingtons for her to put on and her red duffel coat and white hat and scarf and gloves.

'Now, Leah,' said Lucy, holding her hand—she loved how small it was—'you can be a very good little reindeer called

Starlight. Reindeer don't go in rivers do they? Reindeer are very good and stay out of the water.' Leah nodded her head very seriously.

'And Starlight the reindeer has reins,' said Rosie, slipping them over Leah's head.

They all went down the garden through the gate and on to the path by the river.

'We'll need to be careful as the water is a bit higher than normal, but it's still not too deep. If the adults stand in the deepest part and we all have waterproofs

on then I think we can work together in the same spot,' said Gran. 'I've brought some gloves if people need them, and some litter pickers. You just squeeze the handles and the jaws at the end will grab the rubbish. Now, if you give me Leah's reins, Leah can help me hold the bag and everyone can pass me the rubbish. That's a very important job to do, isn't it, Leah? We're picking up all the nasty rubbish that hurts animals.'

At first Leah was very good as they passed the rubbish down, and because they were all working together they cleared a lot. The river itself wasn't too dirty, but in the reeds and

plants at the side there were
crisp packets, sweet wrappers,
and drink cans and their plastic
wrappings.

Leah started fidgeting after a while
so Rosie and Lucy came out of the water
to help hold the bag and keep her happy.

'Let's sing some songs!' said Mum.
'I know—"Jingle Bells"!' So they all sang
'Jingle Bells', and then 'Twinkle, Twinkle,
Little Star'.

'What a lovely voice you have, Rosie,'
said Gran.

'Yes, it's gorgeous,' said Lucy's dad,
smiling and looking very cheerful in
his red Christmas hat.

'We keep telling her that, don't we Leah?' said Peter.

'Thank you!' said Rosie. She went a bit red but looked very pleased.

'How are you feeling now about singing on Christmas Eve?' said Lucy quietly as the others got on with passing the rubbish.

'I was worrying about it all yesterday evening,' said Rosie. 'I know you say I'm good, but I'm still scared about singing in a concert. I'm sure I'm going to forget the words or sing a wrong note. I can't wait for it to be over.'

Lucy felt really sorry for Rosie and wished her friend felt more confident.

Then Leah wanted the reindeer song, but instead of singing 'Rudolf the Red-nosed Reindeer' she wanted to sing 'Starlight the Red-nosed Reindeer'. Leah was doing a funny little dance when Will, who was in the river wearing waders, looked down at his feet and shouted, 'Hey, I can see fish!'

'Me see fish!' shouted Leah, and ran towards the river. Luckily Lucy grabbed her reins so she didn't properly fall in, but she sat down with a bump on the bank, her trousers got very wet, and her wellingtons filled with water. She started to cry as Peter poured the water out of her boots on to the grass and she looked very sadly at her wet socks.

'Naughty river. Naughty water. COLD!' she said.

'Oh dear,' said Peter. 'I think this little reindeer has got a little bit tired. I'll take her back to the house.'

Everybody waved Leah off as Peter carried her back up the garden path.

'I think this stretch of river is pretty clear now,' said Gran. 'Good job, everyone! I'm very pleased to see fish in it—that shows it isn't too polluted.'

'I think we'd better not go back to the house just yet so that Peter can settle Leah down,' said Mum.

'How about a quick football match

and then meet back at Rosie's?' said Dad. 'Anyone up for it if I nip home and grab a ball?'

'I am!' said Sita.

'I think I'd like to walk along the river a little way and see if I can see any signs of otters,' said Gran.

'Can I come?' said Rosie. 'I'm not as keen on football as Sita.'

'Nobody could be as keen on football as Sita—except Oscar!' laughed Lucy.

As Lucy, Rosie, and Gran walked away from the backs of the houses, the river became quieter and more peaceful. They stopped talking and listened to the sounds of the river and the trees beside it—the rustling of birds in hedges, the water as it flowed over some rocks, a duck quacking somewhere.

'Look!' Gran said. 'Did you see that!'

They had all seen a flash of blue.

'That was a kingfisher, girls!' said Gran. 'What a wonderful sight! I love those river birds so much!'

Lucy looked down on the ground.

'Gran—look! I think I see some footprints in the mud by the water's edge!'

'Clever girl! Those are otter prints. And look—some otter spraint. You can see that it has eaten some fish—look at the fish bones. So this is a message to any other otters that this is an otter's territory.'

'I wonder if it is our otter's mum or dad?' said Lucy.

'We can't know, as our cub may have been washed down quite a distance because of the flooding. But at least this river has otters in it—that's a good thing,' said Gran.

'Shall we go home and have some hot chocolate?' said Rosie. 'I'm getting a bit cold now.'

'Me too,' said Lucy.

'I think I'll go home and feed that little otter and give Tom another ring,' said Gran. 'I really want that otter back in the wild as soon as possible. The longer he is away from it and other otters, the harder it will be to get him back there. I'll take this shortcut home now—you go back to Rosie's house, Lucy. Thanks for all your help.'

'I'll come and see you later,' promised Lucy.

It was getting dark by the time Lucy and Rosie got back to the house. They could see the Christmas tree twinkling inside. It looked so welcoming.

When they got through the door

everyone was inside happily talking about the football match. Mum had saved a goal, and Oscar and Sita had both scored one, so they were very pleased. Lucy's dad was complaining because he said Lucy's mum had stopped his goal, and Sita's parents were laughing at him. Oscar, Will, and Fergus were tucking in to the cake Rosie's mum had made. Leah came downstairs smiling after her nap and got in a terrible mess eating her piece of 'choclit log', as she called it. It was delicious, and with hot chocolate was the perfect thing to have after working on the river.

'What a lovely Christmas holiday we are having!' said Rosie's mum, looking round at everyone.

'Mum only thinks that because she doesn't have to sing in front of everyone,' whispered Rosie to Lucy, looking miserable again. 'It's spoiling my Christmas.'

Chapter Six

Lucy went back home as soon as she left Rosie's, changed into her uniform, and went straight over to Gran's. She carefully picked up the little otter out of his playpen. He didn't seem at all frightened now. His fur was so soft and his whiskers tickled her as he wriggled up on to her shoulder, but she caught him and held him firmly so that Gran could check his neck.

'He ate a lot just before you came and his neck is looking so much better!' said Gran. As if to prove it the otter gave a big wriggle and jumped off Lucy's lap, running straight to her wellies and climbing into one. It tipped over with his weight and he squeaked and poked his head out.

'Naughty!' laughed Lucy. Gran picked up the welly and soon the otter was back in his pen.

'He's just a baby,' said Gran, 'but I

really don't want him to get too used to us.'

'He's so sweet and soft and roly-poly,' said Lucy. 'I do wish I could take him home.'

'Oh dear—don't wish for that, Lucy,' said Gran. 'If you are going to wish for anything, wish for him to get a place at the sanctuary. I'm afraid we are both getting too fond of him. One day we'll go together and see some grown wild otters—it's much more magical than having one as a pet.'

Lucy wasn't sure. As she walked home she thought about her magic snow globe. Lucy wondered if it would be wrong to wish on the snow globe to keep the wild otter cub, but she knew deep down it would be and that Gran was right. She felt sad. 'I'll miss him so much,' she said to herself. Luckily, when she got home her own pet, Merry the cat, spent most of the evening purring, curled up on Lucy's lap, which made her feel much better.

Lucy got into bed and looked at the snow globe. She remembered what Gran had said: 'If you wish for anything, wish for him to get a place at the sanctuary.' She could wish on the snow globe for the otter and she could wish on the snow globe for Rosie.

'But if I wish for a place at the sanctuary for him I won't see my little otter again,' Lucy said out loud. 'Anyway, the magic snow globe sent the vet. That probably used all the magic up. I'm sure there aren't any wishes left.'

And she turned her back on the snow globe so she couldn't see its gentle glow, and fell asleep. But in her dreams the little otter was very sad, and then she had a dream that Rosie was crying because of having to sing her solo at the concert. Lucy was glad to get up in the morning. Looking at the snow globe made her feel funny inside.

'I don't think there is room for the snow globe on my table,' said Lucy to Rocky, Merry, and Scruffy. 'I have to wrap lots of presents and I need somewhere to put the sellotape and the scissors. I don't want to knock it on the floor and break it. I'll put it in the cupboard so it is safe.'

She didn't look at Scruffy, Merry, or Rocky when she put the snow globe away. She didn't think they'd understand or agree with her.

'I'm sure there is no magic left in it anyway,' she said out loud, as she closed the wardrobe door.

But she wasn't really.

The next couple of days were very busy.

Merry got in the way as Lucy wrapped presents and wrote cards. Lucy, Sita, and Rosie went Christmas shopping and Lucy bought a beautiful scarf for Mum, some Christmas socks for Dad, a book about football for Oscar, and a book about an animal sanctuary for Gran.

'I can't wait for Gran to open this!' she said to Merry when she brought it home and wrapped it up. Merry patted the sellotape and Lucy remembered how Merry used to play with it when she was a kitten.

'You're still a naughty little cat!' Lucy laughed, and Merry purred and rubbed herself up against her as if she agreed.

Lucy and Sita went back to Rosie's and played with Leah. They told her stories and played skittles and a game where you had to throw hoops over some toys. Leah thought it was wonderful and they played it so often Lucy got quite good at it. Then

Rosie and Lucy went over to Sita's to make mince pies, but it wasn't as much fun as it normally was. Rosie looked tired and worried, and Lucy wondered if it was because of the singing. But somehow, Lucy couldn't think of the words to make Rosie feel better, and Rosie didn't really want to talk about it with her.

Every day, Lucy popped over to Gran's Wildlife Rescue Centre to see the baby otter. Oscar came too on the day before Christmas Eve.

'As soon as Gran finds a place at the sanctuary, the otter really does have to go,' Oscar said when they were walking home after the visit.

'Why does everyone keep saying that?' said Lucy crossly, and stomped off. She hardly spoke to anyone all evening, and she went to bed feeling miserable. The magic snow globe was still in the cupboard, and she missed its gentle glow. She didn't feel very Christmassy without it, but if she took it out she would have to think about wishes. And she really didn't want to.

And then all of a sudden it was Christmas Eve.

'I'll go and check on the otter before the concert, shall I, Gran?' said Lucy to

Gran, who had come over for lunch. 'I won't be long.'

'That would be kind of you,' said Gran. 'Could you check the other animals have enough water too?'

It was nice to be out walking in the quiet, fresh air. It made Lucy happy to think of Father Christmas and his reindeer moving across the world to deliver presents. Lucy thought of all the animals she had helped since she had become Gran's special assistant. Lucy remembered the first baby rabbit and she was glad he was back, snug and cosy with his family. At least she had a lovely rabbit badge on her sweatshirt to remind her of him. She loved wearing the uniform Gran had made her whenever she went to the Centre. It was so special to be Gran's wildlife rescue assistant.

At the Centre, Lucy let the little otter out of his cage and he ran around the pen. He had made a little mess in the cat litter tray, so Lucy carefully lifted it out and emptied it into the bin.

Then she washed her hands and went back to the pen.

But the little otter was gone. Lucy must have nudged the sides of the pen a little when she stepped out, and he must have squeezed himself out the side.

'Oh no!' said Lucy.

Luckily she could hear his excited chittering, and she saw him by the door. But then he turned and she saw his tail disappear through the cat flap. He was out in the dark garden, where there was a pond and all sorts of dangers for a baby otter who hadn't learned to swim.

'What can I do?' said Lucy, grabbing some thick gloves. She looked around

and saw some towels folded in the bottom of a laundry basket. Lucy grabbed a towel to throw over the otter—but then she had an even better idea. She put the rest of the towels on the side, grabbed the empty basket, and ran out.

'Please may he not have gone far,' she said under her breath, looking all around the garden. 'Please may he not get hurt.'

Chapter Seven

The next few minutes felt like hours for Lucy. She looked around the sheds and down the path, but could see nothing. She ran to the pond, because that would be a dangerous place for him, but he wasn't there. Then she spotted him, on the lawn by a garden gnome.

'Magic snow globe, I know you're not here, but please help me!' Lucy said, and threw the basket. As the basket flew through the air Lucy was sure she saw a flash of something like a stream of glittering stars, and heard a gentle tinkling of bells.

The basket landed on the otter and the garden gnome. The otter was trapped! It gave lots of indignant whistles and squeaks, and the basket started to shuffle as the otter tried to get out. The good thing was that, although the basket moved a little, the garden gnome inside made it too heavy for the little otter to

get far. Lucy felt so relieved she wanted to laugh, but she knew there wasn't time— she didn't want him to wriggle out again.

'Lucy—what's happening?' came Gran's voice from the doorway. 'You took such a long time to come home I thought I'd come and check on you.'

'Bring the cat basket, Gran,' called Lucy. 'It's all right—the otter escaped but I've got him under the laundry basket.'

Gran rushed out and together, using the towel, they grabbed the very cross otter cub and got him back in the cat basket.

'Thank you!' said Lucy to the garden gnome as she put him straight and back in his place on the lawn.

The otter was furious that his adventure had stopped, and, when they brought him in and put him back in his cage, he made a lot of noise to tell them so.

'I'm so sorry, Gran,' said Lucy, over the indignant cries. 'He must have squeezed out the side of the pen when I was emptying the litter tray. Then he ran out through the cat flap.'

'All's well that ends well,' said Gran. 'You did a wonderful job catching him. But I think this really proves he needs to be somewhere else. It's just a shame it will have to wait until after Christmas now. Oh well, we've tried our best.'

I haven't, thought Lucy. *I haven't tried my best for the otter and I haven't tried my best for Rosie. I knew deep down I could have wished on the snow globe for them both, but I put it away instead so I wouldn't have to think about it and I could pretend the magic had run out.*

Lucy rushed back home and got the snow globe out of the cupboard. She held it in her hands and sat on the bed with Scruffy and a sleepy Merry.

'Magic snow globe—thank you for helping me catch the little otter. I know he needs to grow up with other otters and go back to the river when he is ready. Please may it not be too late to wish for a place in the sanctuary for the little otter in time for Christmas. I should have wished for that before but I didn't want you to grant my wish. I wanted to keep the little otter forever, but I know that won't make him happy. Oh, and one last thing: please can you also help my friend Rosie—please can you give her the confidence to sing her solo at the concert later.'

The snow globe glowed gently and Rocky gave a gentle rock. Merry purred and she was sure Scruffy's little pyjama-case tail gave a little wag.

Lucy shook the snow globe. 'I wish that the little otter will be with other otters this Christmas, and I wish that Rosie won't feel nervous tonight.'

The snow fell faster and faster on the woodland scene, turning white and silver and red, orange, yellow, green, blue, indigo, and violet. Then the wood disappeared and suddenly there were lots of sparkling patterns in the globe—lots of tiny glittering musical notes and then lots of tiny little otter shapes swimming and turning and rolling together. It was so pretty to watch. The globe felt warm and comforting in her hands, and Lucy felt a tingling fizzy happiness creep from her toes, up to her head, and along her arms. She could imagine just how happy

385

and free an otter felt swimming in the river.

Then the snow turned white again, and the little house and the woods were back.

'I know what I have to do now,' said Lucy, and ran downstairs to ring Rosie.

When Rosie answered she sounded very quiet and sad.

'Rosie,' said Lucy. 'I just want to tell you not to be scared. We will all be there to support you at the concert.'

'I know,' said Rosie. 'But what if it goes wrong?'

'It won't,' said Lucy. 'Remember we have all heard you singing before.

Remember when we cleared the river and everyone said how lovely your voice was. I know you will be great. Just imagine you are singing for Leah—close your eyes and pretend you are singing to her in bed like you always do. Everything will be fine.'

'Are you sure?' said Rosie.

'Completely,' said Lucy.

'Thank you, Lucy—you're such a great friend,' said Rosie. 'I do feel so much better already.'

When Lucy put down the phone she felt so much better too. It suddenly felt like it was properly Christmas at last.

Lucy, Oscar, Gran, and Mum and Dad joined Peter and Nina and Leah and Sita and her family in the residents' lounge to hear the choir sing.

Leah was sitting on her grandad's knee, but she was getting a bit wriggly and loud.

'Do you girls want to come with me and feed the little birdies,' Grandad said, taking Leah's hand. Leah looked very pleased—she loved her grandad and loved him to tell stories about his farm. He was very old now and walked with a stick, but he still had very twinkly eyes, and always looked after the birds in the garden.

They went outside, and checked there were plenty of fat balls and seeds on the bird table. A little blue tit flew away into the dusk as they arrived.

'Look!' Grandad said suddenly, pointing his stick towards the bottom of the garden.

'Doggy!' shouted Leah excitedly.

'What was it?' said Lucy.

'An otter!' smiled Grandad. 'The garden goes down to the river, and some of the fish have been taken from the pond. I thought there might be otters about!'

'So the doggy Leah kept saying she saw was an otter!' said Sita.

'Clever girl!' said Lucy.

'Look!' pointed Leah. 'Reindeer!'

They looked up in the darkening sky and saw a little flashing light moving. Lucy had told Leah a story about Father Christmas's littlest reindeer guiding the sleigh as he flew to deliver presents.

'Starlight!' said Leah proudly, and Lucy gave her a hug.

'That's right!' said Lucy. 'Starlight the reindeer is in the sky helping Father Christmas because it's Christmas Eve!'

'The concert's starting!' called Lucy's mum from the patio doors, and they went back inside. Lucy saw Rosie standing at the front of the choir and remembered her wish on the snow globe again.

'Please may Rosie not be nervous,' Lucy said under her breath.

Just in time Rosie's dad arrived. He waved at Rosie and sat down in the front row.

Then Rosie closed her eyes and began to sing.

Chapter Eight

Rosie's voice sounded wonderful. Even
Leah was quiet. She sat, snuggled up
on her grandad's lap, and sucked her
thumb as Rosie sang the first verse of a
beautiful Christmas carol. When Rosie
had finished her verse she opened her

eyes and smiled, and the choir and the people sitting in the lounge joined in the rest of the verses. Lucy saw Rosie's grandad wipe a happy tear from his eye as everyone clapped the choir at the end. Everyone agreed that Rosie's solo had been the best they had ever heard. Rosie's dad gave her a big hug and Lucy could see how happy that made Rosie. It was special that he had come to hear her too. Peter and her mum came over and they were all smiling and talking together.

'That was marvellous, Rosie love,' Rosie's grandad said, when Rosie gave him a kiss.

'It was wonderful,' said Sita.

'You sounded amazing!' said Lucy.

'Thank you!' said Rosie, beaming. 'And it was a miracle, because I wasn't nervous at all. I just remembered what you told me Lucy, I imagined I was singing to Leah, and I felt confident. Thank you so much.'

'Thank you snow globe,' whispered Lucy under her breath.

'Look—there are homemade mince pies!' said Sita's mum. Oscar and the girls passed them around to everyone, and they drank tea and pulled crackers. Everyone put on Christmas hats and read out jokes from their crackers. Leah insisted on doing a dance in the middle of the lounge, and was very pleased when everyone clapped. She got a bit over excited and didn't want to stop, but luckily Grandad had a parcel to give her, and she was very pleased when she ripped

the paper off and found it was a toy lamb.

'Like the little lambs I had on my farm and kept warm in my kitchen,' smiled Grandad, and gave Leah a kiss.

That reminded Lucy of the otter being warmed up.

The manager of the home gave out Christmas bingo cards. There were lots of pictures of Christmassy things—puddings, donkeys, stars, crackers, and presents—and people had to match them to the cards she would pull out of a hat. It was lots of fun. Then Gran's mobile phone rang.

'That's funny—I thought I'd switched it off,' she said as she took it out of her bag. 'I'm so glad it didn't ring during the concert.'

'Hello? Really? How wonderful! Tonight? That is the best Christmas present you could give me! Thanks, Tom! See your brother in ten minutes then! Bye!'

Gran finished the call with a big smile on her face.

'That was my good friend, Tom, from the otter sanctuary. He says they have a place for the otter! His brother is driving down to visit him for Christmas, and they have realized he will be passing through here in the next half an hour and he can pick up the otter cub on the way. Isn't that wonderful? Our baby otter will be with other otters for Christmas! Do you want to come with me, Lucy, and get him ready for his new home?'

Lucy ran and gave Rosie and Sita a hug and rushed off with Gran.

The otter loudly complained in the warm cat basket Gran got ready for him, even though he had his teddy and hot-water bottle. Lucy smiled at Gran.

'I just hope that he stops making all that noise or Tom's brother will have an awful car journey with him.'

'I think I need a nice cup of tea,' said Gran. 'And I think you deserve one of your presents a little early.'

Gran passed Lucy a little package. Lucy smiled when she opened it and saw what was inside. It was a tiny model of an otter and a new badge for her uniform with an otter on it.

'Thanks, Gran,' Lucy said, and gave Gran a big hug. 'I definitely won't forget how I got this badge!'

Lucy noticed that the otter had gone quiet. *He must have tired himself out with all his complaining*, she thought. Lucy peeped inside the cat basket and saw him curled up next to his teddy, asleep.

'When you wake up you will get a lovely
surprise!' she whispered to him. 'You're
very sweet now but you definitely need to
be with other otters. You're going to learn
to swim and then go back to the wild. You
will have a lovely time! Happy Christmas!'

Tom's brother arrived and was very nice. He stayed and had a cup of tea with them and Lucy told him all about rescuing the otter and how they had cleared out the river of rubbish so another animal wouldn't get hurt.

Then he took the little otter in his cat basket and drove off.

Lucy waved him off. 'Goodbye little otter,' she whispered.

'See you tomorrow, Lucy,' said Gran 'and thank you for being such a wonderful assistant and lovely granddaughter. I love you very much.'

'I love you too, Gran,' said Lucy, and they gave each other a big hug.

When Lucy got home she rang Sita and Rosie to explain what had happened before the concert. They both laughed when she told them about throwing the basket over the otter and they arranged to meet up after Christmas.

Lucy was getting ready for bed when Gran rang with exciting news.

'Tom just called,' said Gran. 'He was so impressed to hear about you clearing the river that he has invited us all down to the sanctuary after Christmas. He is going to give us a special V.I.P. tour and we can see our baby otter and meet the otters he is going to live with.'

'That's so wonderful!' said Lucy. 'I

can't wait to see him in the sanctuary. He is going to have such a lot of fun!'

Lucy took her little otter model and put it next to the snow globe by her bed.

'Thank you for hearing my wish in the garden when the otter escaped,' said Lucy to the snow globe. 'And thank you for working magic again and helping the otter get well. I'm so glad he is going to be safe in the sanctuary and go back to the wild. And thank you for helping Rosie feel confident.'

Then she put on her pyjamas, brushed her teeth, checked that her Christmas stocking was hung up at the end of her bed, and, patting Rocky, got into bed. She put her arms around Merry and Scruffy and went straight to sleep.

It was Christmas morning.

Lucy sat up and looked in her stocking. It was full of lovely things. There was a book called *Tarka the Otter*, some chocolate coins in a little purse with a picture of a baby reindeer on it, and a notebook with a picture of a baby rabbit on it. There was a calendar with otters on it too.

'I can write the date on it that we are going to visit the otter sanctuary!' said

Lucy happily.

There was even a small cat toy for Merry and two ribbons—so Lucy put one on Scruffy and the other she tied around Rocky's neck.

Then Lucy noticed that the magic snow globe was glowing softly and there was a folded piece of paper sticking out from under it. As she pulled it out and opened it there was the sound of sleigh bells and the paper sparkled. The letter was written in lovely big curly writing, and reading it made her feel very, very happy.

Well done Lucy!

The Christmas magic came from you this year. Well done for being such a good kind friend, for making the river safe for the birds and animals, and for saving a very special little otter.

xxx

Then Lucy looked over at the snow globe, and she saw that it was lightly snowing inside, even though she had not shaken it. In the woods she could see a little figure dressed in red with a long white beard who was waving at her. Beside him in front of the cottage was a sweet little reindeer, whose white fur sparkled, and who gave a little jump as if to say 'hello'.

Merry jumped on Lucy's knee and purred loudly, rubbing her head against Lucy's chin. Her fur was so soft and Lucy felt so happy inside that everything was fine.

Lucy looked at the otter model Gran

had given her and felt excited to think of what a wonderful Christmas the little cub would have with the other otters. 'See you soon, my little otter,' Lucy said, and as the snow in the snow globe stopped falling magically by itself, and the little figure in red and the tiny white reindeer disappeared from view, Lucy went downstairs to join her family and begin another wonderful Christmas Day.

Thank you . . .

To my husband Graeme and my children,
Joanna, Michael, Laura, and Christina
for all their love and support.

To Sophy Williams for her lovely illustrations,
and Sarah Darby for her design.

To my agent Anne Clark, and to Liz Cross,
Clare Whitston, Debbie Sims and Gillian Sore, and
everyone from OUP who worked on these three books.

To my friend Liz Race for her inspiring
workshop ideas for school visits.

And to all of the wonderful people who gave me
advice about the animals featured in these books: Rob
McMeeking, Krista Langley from the Wildlife Haven
Rescue and Rehabilitation Centre, Angus Carpenter
from the Wildwood Trust, and Tom Cox at Buckfast
Butterflies and Dartmoor Otter Sanctuary.

About the author

Every Christmas, Anne used to ask for a dog. She had to wait many years, but now she has two dogs, called Timmy and Ben. Timmy is a big, gentle golden retriever who loves people and food and is scared of cats. Ben is a small brown and white cavalier King Charles spaniel who is a bit like a cat because he curls up in the warmest places and bosses Timmy about. He snuffles and snorts quite a lot and you can tell what he is feeling by the way he walks. He has a particularly pleased patter when he has stolen something he shouldn't have, which gives him away immediately. Anne lives in a village in Kent and is not afraid of spiders.

Christmas
wishes
really can
come true
with
Lucy!

ANNE BOOTH

Making a wish for a Christmas miracle.

Lucy's Search for Little Star

Illustrated by Sophy Williams

ANNE BOOTH

Can Lucy save Christmas for a poorly rabbit?

Lucy's Magic SNOW GLOBE

Illustrated by Sophy Williams

Lucy's Secret REINDEER

Illustrated by Sophy Williams

ANNE BOOTH

Christmas miracles come in all sizes

Lucy's Winter RESCUE

Illustrated by Sophy Williams

ANNE BOO

A new arrival just in time for Christmas

Lucy's Magical SURPRISE

Illustrated by Sophy Williams

Here are some other stories we think you'll love!